The Con

ll

Nako

Introduction

"Where did we go wrong? You have yet to answer the million dollar question. Christian, let's be honest with each other here....please, can we be honest with each other. I'm a big girl I can handle it. Just tell me, do you love her? Is that who you want to be with? Because if so, it's okay, just don't string me along anymore. I deserve to be with someone who actually wants to be with me," Farren stated with confidence. In fact it was the first thing she said with confidence all year. Her voice was no longer shaking and she didn't utter or mumble; she spoke with finality. Who wanted to be with someone who barely touched them or made eye contact with them? Who wanted to love a man who didn't love or respect his "woman"? Who wanted to chase and beg someone for simple gestures of affection?

The hardest part of letting go is letting go. Farren believed that she had done all she could do to save their marriage and if it had now come to an end, then she would appreciate the lesson learned and somehow place the pieces of her life back together. But when a man doesn't even hide his side bitch anymore, it's out in the open for friends and family to know but not speak on the situation, then yeah, it's time to leave. Farren was beautiful and she knew it, but after years of researching ways to keep your husband happy, tips on spicing the bedroom up, and other bullshit that could be found on Google, she was over it.

Separating their children or what others thought didn't bother him, and their vows apparently meant nothing to him. Farren had to get her life together. She'd spent countless nights crying and drinking. Her career that she put so much time into was failing, and she was losing case after case. Her dreams were turning into nightmares and she couldn't recall the last time she'd actually put on clothes and enjoyed herself. She wanted her mind and heart back.

She gave him one more chance to answer the question before she decided that she was filing divorce.

"We are not getting a divorce so you can get that out of your head." With that being said, he ended the conversation.
What in the world had she gotten herself into? Who did she marry? She had no idea.

In the beginning, memories are made love fades over time but why?

Farren

The next morning was a blur. Farren ran for her life. She did her morning routine as she normally does, but an irritated feeling in the pit of her stomach was saying, *something is not right.* She turned up her Beyoncé and continued on with her run. When she stopped to take a break and to decrease her heart rate, a man in a black suit was standing near a tree. It wasn't too often you'd see African-Americans in this prestigious neighborhood. With all of this shit going on, Farren was stupid to run without her phone or gun.

She kept her eye on him as she jogged in place, and cracked her neck. Before she knew it, the man was coming out of hiding and Farren took off down the hill, running for her life. Out of nowhere, two more men snatched her up, and before she could scream, a dirty un-manicured hand covered her mouth, forcing her to be silent.

What the fuck did Christian have going on was the only thought that went through her mind, as she was tossed into a van. The van didn't move for at least thirty minutes. Voices could be heard but they were really muffled. She now regretted not bringing a cell phone, knife or something.

She wondered was it the Italians she knew he did business with, was it street niggas or worse, the Feds messing with her again. The agent was worrisome and called her every hour on the hour. Farren began blocking any number she didn't recognize.

She refused to cry; Farren ran with the toughest of the toughest growing up, so if they "thought" she was some dumb ass wife who would just run her mouth or let them kill her with ease, oh boy were they in for a rude awakening. She didn't play that shit at all, but she would give them a chance to speak first before she went off on them for interrupting her morning run. At the moment, her children were her only concern.

Hours later, she was being escorted into what she assumed was a building.

"Why is she blind folded...and y'all have her mouth taped! Are you stupid?" She heard someone fuss behind her.

A foul smelling odor attacked her nose, reeking of balls and cigarettes. Instantly the tape was snatched off her mouth, and her hands were un-cuffed.

"Ms. Walters, Ms. Walters, why must we go through this just to get in touch with you? We called you twice last night." The federal agent from earlier sat across from her in a cold grey room with a metal table.

Farren rolled her eyes and spat, "For the third time, because I am keeping count, if you are not pressing charges, please take me back home where you found me. Now the next this time this happens, I will gladly be requesting a restraining order," she told the agent.

Now that she knew she was in the hands of enforcement, her heartbeat slowed down.

"Look, let me make myself clear. Your husband is going to jail; now you can easily be an accessory to his growing list of charges if you don't work with us. We are here to help you."

"And again, contact my lawyer. I don't know what you are talking about. As far as I am concerned, my husband owns a successful architecture company and does real estate," she smiled.

A dark skinned, plus-sized woman entered the room without a greeting or even a smile. She stood in the corner and observed Farren carefully, but little did she know, Farren was watching her too. She had seen her before, she just wasn't sure where.

"We are to help you. Just tell us who his supplier is," the federal agent said.

"I do not know what you are..." the woman whose skin reminded her of dark chocolate interrupted her.

"Listen here bitch, I'm not going to play with you. Your husband is cheating on you, okay? Here are some pictures because I know you don't believe us. She refused to talk too, and honestly y'all both are stupid. Whoever can come to us first will get a better deal. So what you wanna do?"

"Good morning to you, too," Farren mumbled as she stared at the folder before opening it.

It was as if the folder had bright letters in bold that read, "Pandora's Box." But she pushed that aside, curiosity taking over, and slowly opened the folder. She wanted to ask them for privacy, but she was confident it was a room full of agents watching her every move.

Her heart pounded as she flipped through the folder to see Christian with HER at the park, at a Floyd Mayweather fight, eating sushi, and ordering roses. She couldn't remember the last time she received roses from his ass. Then she remembered Dolly saying something about roses being delivered to her office a few days ago. It was HER; she had stolen her husband, that little slutty tramp. Farren didn't even know if she cared to cry. She attempted to hold her marriage together the best way she knew how, and that was through prayer. What did she do wrong? She suddenly saw spiders all over the pictures and screamed aloud as she dropped them to the floor.

"Ms. Walters, are you okay?" one of the younger agents asked.

Farren opened her eyes again and realized that there weren't any spiders crawling on her now estranged husband and his mistress' pictures. She shook her head as she thought, *this nigga will not drive me crazy.* Where did spiders come from? There weren't any spiders; Farren knew she was tripping.

"Ms. Walters...," she cut him off. "My name is Mrs. Knight. Do not refer to me as Ms. Walters and if that's all you got, then please take me home," she said quietly.

She'd be damned if she'd shed tears in front of these peasants. They were risking their lives for an average of maybe fifty or sixty thousand dollars a year. She just prayed it was worth it because even if Christian didn't have an explanation for the pictures, he was probably going to kill each and every one of them, federal agent or not. They now had fucked up his little happy life, because sweet Farren had instantly become one bitter bitch.

"Drop her off in the hood", the federal agent who had been blowing her phone up and stalking her, instructed the younger one to do.

"Lead the way." She stood to her feet and followed him to his unmarked, blue Impala.

Farren was so angry she didn't know what to do. The agent dropped her off in the middle of Fifth Ward, wearing only a sports bra, leggings and tennis shoes. Although her body was drop dead gorgeous, she still was super shy and timid.

"Excuse me, can I use your phone?" Farren walked into a nail shop and asked the Chinese lady. People were looking at her like she was crazy. Her neighborhood was predominately white, so it was normal to go get the mail in your sports bra and sneakers.

"Christian, come get me right now. I'm on Lynch Street," she yelled as soon as he picked the phone up. She didn't give him a chance to respond. He had exactly ten minutes to come and get her.

Farren completely ignored the stares of the patrons in the nail salon, as she tapped her foot quietly watching the clock and the window.

Thirty minutes later, a black Range Rover was slowly pulling up. She assumed he had been looking for her, but if he was as smart as he claimed to be all the time, he would have known to just call the shop back.

Farren marched to the car and slid in the back seat, once she noticed his best friend Greg, was in the front.

"What happened? Where have you been? It's too much going on for you to be running away and especially with that on." Christian went in once she closed the door and they pulled off.

She counted to ten and tried her hardest not to snap out while Greg was in the car. She leaned her head against the window and didn't say anything.

"I'm talking to you Farren!" he yelled.

She snapped her head up. "I hear you, what do you want me to say? Do you really think I would run away? I'm thirty-nine years old, who the fuck runs away? Let me tell you where I was, at a police precinct. Did you think for once, maybe my wife was kidnapped or killed? Nooo, all you thought was oh she mad because she found out about my lil side bitch," she spoke quietly, but the anger and frustration was evident in her voice.

Christian didn't say anything, but she did notice that he gripped the steering wheel and increased speed once they were on the highway.

"Oh, you have nothing to say, huh, husband of fifteen years, who I gave three children too?" she asked with sarcasm.

He remained quiet, so she continued. "Farren, I'm done with this street shit; that life is behind me. Farren I'm done fucking hoes; Farren baby I didn't give you no STD that's probably some bacteria in your body; Farren why would you get pregnant again, you know I don't want any more children. Ooh, my favorite one, Farren I'm drunk, I can't drive. I'll be home in the morning." She couldn't even say anything else. Her body or heart wouldn't allow her to collectively place words together to speak any more of the hidden truth.

And hidden truth is really dumbing it down. It's more than hidden; it's buried twenty million feet under. Mistakes that he's made that placed her health in danger, along with signs of infidelity that she closed her ears and eyes to. Hurt isn't a word to describe how she felt at the current moment. Death...it felt like death. As much as she loved him, to see him love and smile with another woman, gave her the feeling of death.

Farren wiped tears back, and YET, he said nothing. His best friend said nothing. She would do anything to know what thoughts ran through his head right now.

One would think that Christian would have dropped Greg off then went home to make up and salvage what was possibly left of their marriage, but no, he pulled the truck into their spiral driveway and unlocked the door.

"Really?" she asked. "You really gon drop me off at home, like we have nothing to discuss?" She just wanted to clarify this situation. Farren knew she wasn't leaving her husband, no matter what he did. Who was she without him?

"Man get out, I got shit to handle. I'll see you when I get back and when the kids come from school, please take all that crying to your bedroom," he hissed.

Not one "sorry", "we're going to talk about this", "them folks lying", he didn't bother to explain himself at all. Farren tried to conclude what his actions meant. Did that mean he didn't care? Or did he have a long day and had truly been worrying about her? When a man doesn't talk, is it what he doesn't say that's most important or what he does say? She was confused, hurt, lost, and scared.

The idea of Christian leaving her never crossed her mind. I mean yeah, they had a few minor issues, but him leave her for a stripper? It wouldn't happen...it couldn't happen...or could it?

What was her reality? What was their future? Damn, for the first time in years, Farren questioned the position in her husband's life.

"Farren..." Christian turned around and his eyes met hers. She searched them for sadness or regret, yet she saw nothing. Her chink eyes filled with tears that fell because she had no control over her feelings right now.

"I have somewhere to be baby, can you please get out?" he softened his tone and asked her once more.

She wanted to ask him did he love her but embarrassment stopped her. She mentally told herself to remove herself from his car and run away, but the reality of the situation was she went into her home, cleaned up and cooked a dinner fit for a royal family. She walked around in a daze until her children came home. The Stepford smile and waving arm met them at the bus, as she asked them about their day and assisted with homework. In the back of her mind, she counted down the hours until she could tell them it was bedtime, go into Christian's secret stash and roll her up a fat ass blunt, then envisioned herself drinking Patron and putting the pieces of the puzzle together. There was no way in hell she was about to lose her husband, and to a stripper at that.

Christian

"Nigga, I thought Farren was about to pop your ass," Greg shouted once Farren FINALLY got out of the car; it took her about twenty minutes.

When he finally was able to exhale, he wiped his forehead.

"Me too, I can't even lie."

"How does she know about Asia?"

"My phone must have fallen out my pocket and a text message popped up from her, but I'm like damn, how do you remember her name all those years ago? That was a long ass time ago, and everything happened so fast," he rambled.

"She sounds mad... what you gon do?"

He didn't have an answer to that question. "I really don't know, man. You know I love my wife."

"And you fuck with Asia."

"Yeah, but I wouldn't leave my kids for her or nothing like that," he tried to convince himself. He hated all of this has happened. He thought he did a great job keeping both homes happy.

"You sure about that my dude?"

No...yes...maybe? He was too old to be acting like he was drunk in love, so he kept the real answer to himself. He could only imagine how many strands of hair Farren had pulled out by now. He thought, *my poor baby. I'll have to make sure I get home early to fuck her good enough.* Christian was praying for a miracle at this point.

"I don't feel like dealing with her dramatic ass. I have enough problems right now," he told Greg.

"I knew it was coming. We've been running around like we twenty-five again," Greg laughed.

"No, you been running around like you twenty-five, I be in the house," he stated, but wasn't laughing at all.

Christian was considered the Connect; but the Connect had to be connected to something and that "something" was deadly, powerful, and bizarre. He was now on his way to a meeting. The "meetings" didn't happen often.

An hour and a half later, he was powering his phone off and taking two steps at a time to take a seat on the small plane that Alonso had sent for him. He silently prayed to himself that he returned home to his family in one piece. He was unaware of what they were meeting about, but he had an idea: a rat. Whoever was ratting in the camp had to be dealt with, immediately. Christian had only taken this trip a few times over the years, and a few being three. Each of those trips were all celebrations to commemorate the success of the empire. Only one person knew he took the trips; not Farren, not his best friend and business partner, Greg, nor his favorite sister and confidante, Courtney. For some odd reason, he only trusted HER. She was the one who understood why he still did what he did, even though he had surpassed wealth.

"Where is Asia? She didn't want to see me?" Alonso joked once Christian's feet touched Miami soil. The private jet took him directly to Alonso's backyard.

"She had a nail appointment and didn't want to miss it, you know how girls are." He offered him a firm handshake.

"And how is the wife, what's her name again?" Alonso asked, attempting to play dumb. And Christian didn't appreciate him playing him like a fool.

"Farren, and she's well but I'm sure you already knew that. I'm trying to get home before dinner, so what's up?" He ended all pleasantries.

Christian had no plans of having a drink or taking a walk on the beach. His plan was to have this conversation quickly, before the pilot could even finish turning everything off properly.

"Christian, you're going to have to step back in and handle this rat," Alonso spoke firmly.

"I was told to step down, now I'm being asked to get my hands dirty?"

"No one asked you, that's a direct order."

"From who?"

Christian and Alonso's relationship had grown over the years and he considered him a great friend. But truth be told, Alonso was all bark and no bite; it was his father who really lived the life.

"Come on Christian, why so hostile? You know how this goes: kill the problem or get cut off. What does that rapper say...straight like that!" Alonso let out a hearty laugh, and his guards joined in as if on cue.

Christian cut his eyes and turned around to head back to the plane.

"One week, make it happen," Alonso shouted and received no response back. This petty ass conversation could have been had over a throw away phone.

He didn't return back to Philly until late. Instead of going straight home and resolving all issues with his wife, Christian drove around the streets; something he did to clear his mind. The gutter...he had to get down and dirty with these young niggas, to find out what was going on.

He knew it was time for him to carry his ass home once he heard the late night radio show's theme song. As tired and clouded as his mind was, he prayed to every God there was that Farren's ass was good and drunk because he was not in the mood to argue.

And for some reason, thirty minutes later once he secured the alarm and heated him up a hot plate of teriyaki chicken, cabbage, mashed potatoes and cornbread, he was happy to find out that his family was asleep, and Farren was in bed with Noel and Carren. Christian made a mental note to drop an offering off at the church he grew up in, first thing Sunday morning.

The next morning, Christian woke up to an empty house. It was a quiet Saturday morning at the Knight's residence. He reached for his phone to call his wife when he remembered last night's events and thought against it. He scanned his phone to return the one missed call that slipped his mind...Asia. He began to reminisce on the crazy night they'd first met.

About Four Years Ago in Atlanta, Georgia

"Baby, when are you coming home?" Farren asked me. I had been visiting several cities to see what the competition looked like. Although I was "The Connect", legit businesses were my passion; to take a thought and transform it into a vision, draw it out to create a blueprint and then six months to a year later, see the vision transformed to a reality. WOW! That's amazing to me. I had plans to expand my business in the South before tackling other regions, so what better place to start then Atlanta?

"In a few days. What the kids doing?" I looked at my watch while waiting on my wife to wrap this conversation up. You know how most people would catch the hint that you were busy or didn't feel like talking? Yeah, Farren never caught the hints or the signs. She would hold the phone as long as she could.

"They're doing well. Noel is getting into everything, I'm about to start back whooping her. I cooked a meatloaf today, I have a hair appointment in the morning…"

I cut her off, "baby let me call you back. Let me order some room service before it's too late."

She remained silent for a few seconds then smacked her lips. "Call me back, don't forget"

"I'm not," I told her.

"I love you," she said.

"I know, I'm going to call you right back," I said and hung the phone up before she could start another conversation. I love my wife, God knows I do, but damn! I would be lying if I said I was rushing back home to a nagging wife. She didn't nag on purpose and it wasn't intentional; she was just naturally over-concerned.

I took a shower after ordering a T-bone steak from the W hotel where I had been residing for the past few days. I picked up the phone and called my homeboy from college to see what was going on in Hotlanta on a Monday night.

"Christian mother fuckin Knight, the smoothest of the smooth, what do I owe the pleasure of this call?" Barry joked.

"I'm tryna get like you my man," I joked back.

"What it do man, fam good? You good?" he asked, genuinely concerned.

"Yeahhh, we good. I had another daughter about a year ago. I think I'm done for real this time," I told Farren that Noel would be our last child and I meant it.

"Nigga please!" he laughed.

"I'm in yo city, and I've been working nonstop since my plane touched down. I'm trying to get a drink, see some ass. I haven't been to Atlanta in years. What's popping tonight?"

"Shit man, everything popping. You should slide through this lil' laid back spot called Cheetah. The bitches in there look like all they do is squats."

"That sounds like something I'm interested in. What time you want to fall through?" I asked.

"My wife ain't playing that shit; I'm in the house my man. I'll text you tomorrow and we can go get a drink," Barry said.

"Fa sho," I said and disconnected the call.

I had no problem hanging out by myself. A man who depended on others for happiness was a man without a mind. And without your mind, who were you?

Sliding on tailored slacks, a button down and navy Cole Haan's, after asking valet where the club was, I revved up the rental car up and headed to my destination.

Never one to cause much attention, I sat in the back of the club and vibed to the music, sipping a glass of Hennessy. An old school joint came over the speakers; t was a while since I'd heard that song.

The deejay announced over the speakers, "Coming to the stage, women hold your husbands tighter tonight, fellas get ready to make it rain...Midnight they ready for you." I didn't bother looking up. I was enjoying the vibe of the club, entertaining thoughts of possibly looking into opening a strip club; it was clearly a money machine. "Damn, that bitch thick as fuck," I heard someone sitting next to me, say. I looked up to see the beauty on the stage. "Damn," I said aloud. She had the body of a stallion. I was never into tattoos, but her body was covered in art. I wouldn't even call it ink because it looked like it told a story.

She closed her eyes as if no one else was in the building, and began slow grinding to the beat, snapping her fingers. She didn't start dancing until she was good and ready. She didn't beg for money or do insane things with her legs and pussy, she just vibed. I enjoyed her show and before I knew it, I was taking my thirsty ass up to the front for a closer view. I cocked my head and stared at her twerking her backside and wondered if her ass was real. Shit, even her face was pretty; this girl wasn't ugly at all.

Everybody knew I loved the strip club. I would go in there and easily spend ten to twenty thousand, and I had made my mind up that tonight, Ms. Midnight would be getting all my coins. She ended her show with a split and a few more pussy popping moves. I grabbed a waitress and asked for Midnight. She rolled her eyes but after I tipped her twenty dollars, she moved a little quicker. I hated money hungry women; they don't put pep in their step until they see that green dollar bill.

I ordered another drink and decided then, that would be my last one. I had plans for Ms. Midnight and it included having her bent over the edge of my hotel bed, screaming my name. "How can I help you tonight sir?" she asked, sitting on my lap.

She wasn't hesitant and I wondered for a split second did she fuck all her patrons. "I want you to leave with me," I told her calmly.

I wasn't a man that played games or beat around the bush. I said exactly what I thought and spoke with confidence on what I felt. "Oh you got the wrong girl, better ask one of these other bitches," she spoke loudly and lifted her leg to get off my lap.

I grabbed her thigh gently, not too rough; I didn't want her to feel like I was being rough. "Relax... let's talk." I placed her leg back around my waist and leaned back in the suede chair.

"Man wassup, because you don't know me and I don't know you," she said with attitude.

"You're a little feisty, I like it though," I smiled at her.

"Where are you from? Cus I know you not from around here," she asked.

"Philadelphia, up north," I told her.

"Yo, get out of here me too! What hood?" she asked. Her teeth weren't up to my standards, but she had some beautiful eyes and her figure was banging.

"I'll tell you if you tell me your name?" I flirted. She was trying to converse and I was trying to get her to leave with me.

"Midnight, you heard the deejay." she got comfortable sitting in my lap face-forward.

"Let's go," I told her to see what she would say. If she didn't budge then I was headed back to my hotel. I had a beautiful wife at home; I didn't have to chase pussy at all.

She looked me in my eyes, and scanned me over once more. I wondered did she find what she was looking for. I wanted to warn her that I wouldn't be her come up, her sugar daddy, or a nigga she could get over, but she would figure it out in the morning when she woke up and I was already checked out, headed back to my home.

"Okay, let me get my stuff." She hopped off on my lap, and readjusted the thong that found itself hidden in her behind. The ride back to my hotel room was a quiet one other than the ringing of my phone. I knew it was Farren calling, and knowing what she wanted, I quickly answered.

"Babe, you never called me back," she said as soon as I pressed accept.

"I ate and took a shower, then met Barry at the strip club," I told her.

"Oh okay, I haven't heard his name in forever. Is he still married to that girl?" she asked. Farren was so nosey it was ridiculous.

I laughed, "Yes he is. Why aren't you asleep?"

"I'm wrapping up some notes, I have court in the morning," she yawned.

"Get some rest baby, I'll be home tomorrow," I told my wife.

"Okay, I'll have dinner cooked for you, your favorite. I love you so much Christian Knight," she said and I knew she meant it. I had the best wife ever; loving, supportive, prayerful, doting and she was an amazing mother.

"I love you more. Call me in the morning and lock up Farren, don't forget." I had to remind Farren sometimes that even though we stayed in a million dollar neighborhood, she still had to lock the front door, she had become extremely careless over the years and it bothered me.

"Okay baby, I will. Goodnight," she said and hung the phone up.

"Married?" Midnight asked.

"Happily," I replied back. I would not be leading her on or even lying about who I loved. My wife was the SHIT!

"So happily you practically begged me to come to your hotel room tonight?"

I laughed. "Don't you think you're over exaggerating, and I asked you once. I can always turn around and take you back, I'm sleepy anyway." I wasn't playing any games with this girl.

"Why do men cheat? I don't get it," she asked.

"Cheating involves feelings that I don't have. This is about to be a fun night that I won't think about any more after tomorrow," I told her honestly.

She shook her head and wagged her finger as we pulled up to the hotel valet stand. "I'm about to change your life and you don't even know it," she winked.

"Girl, please, come on the elevator is this way," I led her to the private elevator.

On the elevator, I scanned my email for new contracts. "So what do you do?" she asked after mentally adding up my diamond earrings, vintage Audemar Piguet and exquisite shoes.

"I design buildings," I replied without looking up from my phone.

"How long have you been married?"

"Eleven years, I have three children, I graduated from college, I'm six-two, I wear a size twelve in shoe, I love steak and lamb, and I drink Hennessy; anymore questions, Midnight?" The elevator dinged, forcing her to have nothing to say in return.

I stood in front of the door. "My feet hurt, come on," she complained.

"You know what's about to happen, don't you?" I asked. I wasn't in the position to have woman screaming rape on me.

"I'm grown, now open the door"

I nodded my head, slid the key through the slot and opened the door, letting her in first.

"Nice room... where is the shower?" she asked. I pointed in the opposite direction and sat on the couch to roll up some sticky while she handled her business. After two blunts and watching ESPN, shawty finally resurfaced.

She grabbed the blunt out of the ashtray and lit it. "You not scared you gon get caught for smoking in here?" she asked. I looked at her face to see if she was serious, and she was.

I let out a hearty laugh. "Enjoy your smoke, don't worry about that." She clearly didn't know who I was.

"So how often are you in Atlanta?" she asked.

"Why did you move here?" I ignored her question and asked her one instead.

"My boyfriend got locked up. I just needed a breath of fresh air." She took a pull on the joint.

"That's enough for you, come here." I had been waiting on her for an hour, impatiently. It was now time to get to it.

She sat on my lap and started kissing my neck. I wanted to stop and tell her it would be no foreplay, but she was feeling so good.

"I don't normally do this," she said as she licked my earlobe. I rolled my eyes and thought to myself, "bitch please", but I would let her live in her fairytale.

I stood up as she held on to me, and put her on her feet. "Take your clothes off," I told her.

"You're not going to cut the lights off?" she asked.

"No, I want to see you." Again I thought to myself, I do not know you. If you even think you about to pull a gun or knife on me, it was going to be a wrap; but unbeknownst to her, I had already checked her duffle bag when I sent her in the store to get condoms on the ride over here.

She removed her t-shirt and leggings. "Slow down," I told her. I stared at her as I removed my own pants and belt. She was sexy as hell, a few scars here and there but that's what growing up in Philadelphia did to you. I definitely understood that struggle.

She stood there nervously. "You good?" I asked.

"This really is my first time doing this, you thought I was lying?" I stopped thinking with my dick just for a second, as I walked over to her and looked into her eyes. She just might be telling the truth after all.

"Relax, I got you," I told her.

"Do you have any liquor?" she asked.

"Put your clothes back on sweetie." My dick went soft; I wasn't pressed for any pussy. Knowing my wife, she would have hers on a silver platter once I returned home.

"I'm okay, let's do this," she clapped her hands. I laughed; she was too cute. "It's cool, let's finish this blunt." I sat back down in my Burberry boxers and undershirt.

She sat beside me, and for hours we talked about everything. I normally didn't pillow talk but she was cool as hell. We laughed, got serious, had a minor disagreement about the Lakers but overall, I enjoyed her company.

Before I knew it, the phone was ringing. I was an early bird so it didn't bother me at all.

"Hello?"

"Sir, checkout was at ten-thirty, would you like to add another night at the W hotel?" the hotel attendant asked.

I looked over at Midnight and wondered if I was ready to go to home. The angel in me said, "You have a beautiful wife, check out and go home". But my dick jumped at the sight of her ass in those leggings and said, "man stay here one more night and see if you can hit".

"Sir," the hotel attendant called out, I had blanked out for a second.

"Uh, yes, one more night is fine, thank you," I said and hung the phone up. I took a shower and headed out of the bathroom naked, as I looked for a pair of boxers.

"Well good morning to you too." She peeked her head under the throw blanket I had wrapped around her before I retrieved to my room last night, or should I say early this morning.

"I would cover up, but you see me now," I laughed.

"Hmmm…." she said.

"Come here," I told her and went back to the bathroom. As I brushed my teeth and washed my face, she walked in and peed right then and there.

"You just real comfortable around me, huh?" I teased.

She ran shower water and as she waited until it got hot, she bit her lip and stared at me.

"Wasup Midnight?" I knew she enjoyed the sight.

"It's Asia," she spoke, but I couldn't hear her because she had already closed the glass door and stepped into the shower.

I opened it and said, "What did you just say?"

"My name is Asia," she answered me sexily.

I licked my lips and pinned her to the granite marble wall. She jumped due to the wall being cold, but I wouldn't let her move. I kissed her and the kissed surprised me. Although I stepped out here and there, I haven't kissed another woman other than Farren in years. Shit like kissing and head led women to think there was more going on than it was.

She moaned and kissed me back, her sounds encouraging me to continue. I found my way in between her legs and I set a mental goal to get her to cum at least three times before I even entered her.

"Shit!" she screamed as my fingers twirled inside of her. She was as tight as a bunched up fist. I could only imagine what she felt like.

"You like that?" I whispered into her ear and kissed her neck.

She nodded. "No, tell me you like it," I said.

"I LIKE IT, I LIKE IT, I LIKE IT, OMG," she screamed, releasing her love on my hands. I was satisfied.

Round two had just begun. I pinched her nipple and kissed her roughly. I jerked her head back and bit her neck, then stuck one, two, three fingers inside of her and used my thumb to make her clit jump. She squirmed under my touch, and I literally watched the energy drain from and her. That's when I knew I won. Her body had told her it was okay for her to cum once more, and she obeyed. I entered her before she could catch her breath. "Fuck, is this real?" she asked, her eyes rolling back to the head. The beads of sweat forming on her forehead had her looking good enough to eat, but she wasn't my wife. Damn, I entered her raw. Oh well, this pussy tight and wet, I would be a fool to pull out right now. I silently cursed myself for being such a nigga. I should have just stayed home last night; hours later I was in a shower butt ass naked, banging a stripper's back out. "Hmm, this pussy feels so good," she exclaimed, snapping me out of my thoughts. I refocused on the beauty before me and I stroked her slowly. What was wrong with me? I didn't choke her or call her a little dirty slut. I caught myself treating this girl with grace. I was really taking my time with her. Oh hell nah, this pussy had me slipping, literally. It was so wet, I could barely stand up. I was dipping in and out of her honeycomb. She had me feeling like I was twenty-one again.

"Cum with me baby." She looked in my eyes and I had to close mine to keep from catching feelings. Minutes later, I pulled out and watched my nut go down the shower drain.

We both stood breathless. I had nothing to say, but girl
where that pussy come from? Can I get a jar of it to take
back with me to Philly?

She stood ashamed and worried. "I enjoyed you," I told her.
I washed the lust and sin off of me and left her in the
bathroom. After checking my phone, I got dressed quietly
and started packing my bag.

"So that's it?" she asked.

I nodded my head. "Yes, but it was amazing. Don't look so
sad", I told her.

"What about me?" she asked.

"What do you mean sweetheart?"

"I want more," she said, and she was dead ass serious.

I laughed, "I'll call you whenever I'm in the city, give me your
number." I would have given her the number to my business
line but she already seemed a little needy, and I didn't need
her blowing me up at all times of the night.

After I reassured her I would call soon, I headed to the
airport and went back to my wife.

I didn't know at the time that she would grow to become
such an important part of my life. "Hi boo, wasup?" she
answered coolly.

"Shit, just waking up. What's good?" Christian asked, still
rubbing sleep out of his eyes and heading to the kitchen for
a bottle of water.

"Leaving the gym. I texted you last night. I think the dog is
sick, he's been shitting everywhere," she fussed.

"I'll be over there later to see what's going on. I'ma call you back." Christian ended the call when he saw his son playing the game.

"Where is everybody?" he asked.

"Ma took the girls to the spa and stuff," he said, never looking at him.

"You wanna ride with me or you good?" Christian asked his son. "Jerome coming to get me later," he spoke of his oldest nephew who was in his last year of college.

"Okay, I'm going to leave you some money on your dresser before I dip," he hollered as he went back to his room. Christian saw a bag packed and knew that Farren was probably going to Atlanta. She always ran when she didn't want to face a problem. But with school getting out soon, Christian saw it best for her to take the girls with her so he could clear up all loose ends.

He dressed comfortably in a white polo V-neck, basketball shorts and gym shoes. "I'm out son, keep that cell phone charged." He kissed his head, went to power up his Camaro, and decided to call his nephew. "What up Unc?" he whispered into the phone.

"Long night playboy," he joked with his oldest nephew.

"Very long night. I know Mike waiting on me, I'ma go scoop him when I get out the bed," he assured.

"Oh nah, I know you will. He into the game right now, I don't think it's no rush. Do you need any money? I gave your ma some money to send you the other week," he asked. He was all for education and his nephews and nieces all handled their business accordingly. Kennedy, his niece, was finishing up her second year at Spelman and he couldn't be more proud of her. She was basically him and Farren's daughter until they had Carren.

"Unc I'm good," he told his uncle. They ended the call right when Christian was pulling up to his sister's house. He sat in the car for quite some time before getting out. Years ago, Courtney was in an unhappy marriage and really was in love with Christian's best friend Greg, but he didn't want a wife or children. After Courtney's husband found out about the affair, he divorced her and gained custody of their two sons Jerome and Derrick Jr., and their daughter Kennedy. Courtney went into a state of depression which forced her to miscarriage the baby that was conceived out of wedlock, and she lost everything that she loved which was her family. That was years ago and she hasn't been the same since. She'll go days without eating or answering the phone. Kennedy and the other kids were so young that they didn't understand. Their father is all they know and it kills Christian's family on the inside, because despite how she felt about her husband, she loved her children until the end of time.

Christian used his key to let himself in. He smelled coffee brewing and fixed himself a cup. "Brother, what are you doing here?" she asked with a smile. It seemed as if Courtney was having a good day today and for that, Christian was thankful. "Just checking on my favorite sister," he smiled and kissed her cheek.

"I'm well, Crissy, I have a date tonight," she winked.

He laughed, "Girl with who?"

She hesitated. "Greg said he wants to get me out the house." She looked at him for acceptance.

Christian revealed no emotion. He loved his best friend, he really did, but he was growing tired of him playing with his sister's emotions. Courtney would get so worked up and excited about spending time with Greg only for him to not show up because he was handling business or something like that. His sister wasn't mentally stable, in his opinion, to deal with rejection.

Christian changed the subject. "I talked to Jerome today; him and Michael are hanging out," he told his sister.

"He's in town and didn't tell me?" She looked so sad. Over the years, Courtney was pushed out by Derrick and his family to the point where the children's relationship with their mother was strained.

"We're having something at the house tomorrow, so you'll see him there," Christian hurried and made up something. At the rate him and Farren were going, he was going to have to beg her to cook.

"Can we talk?" Christian asked his sister. Despite how others viewed Courtney, she was the ONLY person who knew his inner thoughts and secrets. He loved his sister something serious.

"You're the highlight of my life. Please tell me your problems," Courtney laughed.

"I'm fuckin up," he exhaled.

"What you mean?" she asked.

"Farren found about Asia," he told her.

"AGAIN?" she yelled.

"And the cops are all on my ass and hers," he continued.

"And last night Farren asked me if I was where I wanted to be, which was home with her and my kids, and I just went to sleep. Then Ma keep dropping these remarks like, get your house in order, don't leave your family for fun, Farren is amazing to you, blah blah" he went on and on.

"Okay, one subject at a time. What's up with you and Asia? Do you love her or you just fuckin?" His sister asked the million dollar question.

"Sis, I don't know. She just cool as hell..." she cut him off.

"And you met her in a strip club; you love charity cases. Why do you insist on changing everybody's life, captain save a hoe?" she said, pushing buttons.

"Don't be disrespectful," he hissed. Asia was a sensitive topic for him.

"So what are you going to do, throw your life away just so you can lay up with her? Do you and Farren still have sex?" she inquired.

He looked at her like, really, you gon ask me that. "Every damn day, but it's not about the sex."

"So what other reason has Farren given you to step out on her?" she asked.

"I have no reason," Christian admitted.

"If she's worth you losing your family then so be it," she said and walked off.

Courtney's opinion was appreciated, but unwanted; especially today when he had a lot of shit on his mind. He decided to call his girl and see what she was up to.

"Hey baby," she answered the phone.

"Where you at?"

"Home, I told you I was in the house today"

"You ate?"

"Fruit and water this morning," she said.

"Okay, get dressed, I'm on the way." Christian called Farren to see where she was before he decided on where he and Asia would eat, but she didn't answer the phone. Three exits later, he was illegally parked, waiting on Asia to come downstairs. She finally came down and slid into the passenger seat looking like MONEY. After taking a million trips to Atlanta, he'd told her she needed to move to Philadelphia because he couldn't keep coming up there once a month. He remembered the day just like it was yesterday, even though it was only two years ago.

We were headed to the airport to drop me off as Asia whipped her brand new Audi in and out of the lanes. In so many words, I had upgraded my lil' side piece. I hated to call her that but when it all boiled down to it, that's what she was. In a short time, she captured just a TINY piece of my heart. It was never to be confused how I felt... I loved Farren more than anything. She never failed me as a wife and as a mother, but somehow, someway I had become greedy.

I began to expect more, not from her, but from me. I couldn't explain my feelings or what I was doing. I only felt bad when I returned home to my family and they would come running to the door, missing me, my wife included. She never suspected anything. Farren was confident in her position as my wife and she never once questioned me about my frequent trips to Atlanta. To cover my tracks, I ended opening a tapas bar. I had enough money to open up a bullshit business just so I can have an excuse to get away. I can admit I was getting sloppy lately. Whenever Asia would text me saying she missed me or there was a movie she wanted to see, I would get out of bed and prepare for my trip; but I would wait and tell Farren something came up at the restaurant and I had to fly out immediately.

Asia had a lot to learn about me and she learned quickly. I liked to be in control. I told her, her attitude needed to be checked and she quickly toned it down. She then made an appointment to see the best dental surgeon Atlanta had to offer. Her gap was closed and her bottom row fixed. I asked her to remove all of the extensions and she went and got this sexy ass short cut that I loved on her. She dropped the stripping gig and enrolled in some classes while overseeing the bar for me in my absence. Asia was submissive but she still remained her, and she had no problem checking me if need be.

"Bae, we need to talk." I turned the radio down.

"What?" she asked.

"I think you should move back home..." before she could fuss, I continued. "Wherever you wanna stay, I'll make it happen, but I can't keep taking these trips," I told her honestly. My children were getting older and I was beginning to spend too much time from home, and I didn't like it.

"Chrissy," she said calling my nickname, and I could tell she was annoyed.

I hate that she called me that. I felt like she didn't start calling me that until she heard my wife saying it when I had her speaker phone one day.

"I like Atlanta, no, I love Atlanta. I'm not moving back to Philly to tiptoe around you and your family. Atlanta is my domain," she fussed.

I wasn't hearing shit she was saying. I got my way regardless.

In a few months, I was dropping off the security deposit and paying her rent up for a year.

Christian snapped out of his thoughts as she reached across the console for a hug.

"Look at you," he joked.

"I just threw this on." She threw her hand up and I knew she was lying, because it took her thirty minutes to come down the steps.

"What you have a taste for?" he asked her.

"It don't matter" she said, texting her on cell.

"Put that phone up, today is our day."

He wanted to tell her that Farren knew all about her and it was some shit going on, so she needed to keep her ass of Instagram. However, he just needed a peace of mind on today and with her, everything was right.

"Whatever you say daddy." She tossed her phone in her Chanel bag and leaned back in her seat, getting comfortable.

They grabbed lunch at some Italian spot and caught a movie before heading back in.

"You staying here tonight?" she asked, after a few more hours had passed.

Truth be told, he was hoping when he got home, Farren would already be sleep.

"Nah, let me head on my way; come lock the door," he said, sliding back into his shoes before grabbing his keys.

"You good?" he asked her as they stood in the foyer of her 1600 square feet home.

Even though she had more than enough in her account, he wanted her to know that whatever her heart desired was hers. Christian had just gotten her another car; a bad ass, candy apple red Mercedes Benz that she only drove on the weekends.

"I'm good. Let me know you got home safe." She kissed him on the lips before he dipped out.

Every single light was on in the house, and he knew that Farren and the kids were up

Christian unlocked the door, prepared to deal with his crazy ass wife.

"Daddyyyyyyyy," Noel ran to him and jumped into his arms.

"It smells good in here."

"Mommy is teaching me and Carren how to bake. We made brownies and sugar cookies," she rambled.

"Hi daddy," Carren said, barely looking up from her cell phone.

Farren never looked up from rolling cookie dough. He didn't know if he should speak or not; for a millisecond, he didn't even know how to approach his wife.

"Daddy, you smell good," Noel said.

Farren looked up and her bloodshot eyes met his. They weren't filled with tears but you could tell she had been a sad case today.

She stormed off. "Mommy, where you going?" Noel asked. "Carren, clean this kitchen up and y'all get ready for bed. We're going to grama house tomorrow for dinner," Christian instructed his daughter.

"We wasn't done baking though," she said.

"Yes y'all are," he told her and cut the oven off before entering him and Farren's bedroom. Farren sat at her vanity table, braiding her hair down before she prepared for bed.

"How was your day?" Christian asked.

She grunted, "Oh now you want to talk?"

He shook his head; it was always an argument with her. "I don't wanna talk about that tonight, I just don't."

"Christian, I just found out you are cheating on me and not just cheating, it's a possibility you love this bitch!" she yelled and threw her brush in his direction.

"Farren, shut up," I yelled back.

"Don't tell me to shut up, you shut the fuck up you lying ass bastard." She then threw the remote. Her face was flushed with tears and he could have sworn he saw the devil in her eyes.

"You might as well cancel that hoe, cus I'm not going no mother fuckin where," she said pointing her finger in his face and pushing his head back.

Christian bit his lip because as mad as she had made him by throwing shit, he wanted to slap her.

"Do you hear me?" she asked.

He stared at her, wondering what was wrong with him; this woman was perfect. She had no flaws, she did everything perfect; not one stretch mark, not one blemish. She looked like an Angel in distress and everyone that ever came into her presence instantly loved her. Farren was a sight for sore eyes.

"I said do you hear me? I didn't stand by your side all these years for you to think the next bitch gon get you. Dead that situation before I'm forced to do it for you," she threatened. He knew she wasn't playing but if only she was calm enough for him to explain to her what happened and why. But then really, what would he tell her? That he could confide in her because she listened without talking or offering her opinion? He liked her because she didn't try so hard to please him? He was Farren's world and knew it, and he used to love that about her, but at this present moment he pitied her.

"I'm not dealing with this bullshit Christian, I am not," she cried and fussed.

"Please just go to sleep, you're giving me and you a headache," he told her. She had really gotten on his nerves for tonight; she was the real drama queen, crying instantly and catching temper tantrums.

She was on a rampage tonight. "That's the same bitch from the strip club. You fell in love with a stripper," she laughed, but it wasn't her normal fun sexy laugh; it was filled with venom.

"She was not stripping that night for the last time." Farren thought she knew everything but she didn't. That night when she almost killed the poor girl, she put on a little fit to do something special for him.

"Why are you defending this bitch? Do you love her? Oh what, you been promising her you was going to leave me?" she questioned.

"I wonder did she tell you the Feds talked to her too. They trying to get her to tell on your dumb ass. Whoever talks first gets the deal. Is this bitch loyal?"

Christian didn't know that and wondered why Asia didn't tell him. He would be going back over there first thing in the morning but in the meantime, he had to get Farren's ass to shut up so he could go to sleep.

"Farren stop yelling and cursing at me, now you gon show me some respect. Get in bed and go to sleep. If I tell you the truth you're going to be mad okay, so just stay in your little fairytale." He hated to talk to her like that but it was the truth.

She looked up at him and held his chin in her hand, tight. She stared into his eyes and he looked away. She brought his face to hers, trying to peep into his soul, his mind. It was obvious that she desperately wanted answers. Answers that he knew would hurt her to the core, and he loved her too much to be truthful.

Tears fell from her eyes that she didn't bother to wipe away. She wanted him to see the pain he'd caused in a matter of forty-eight hours. Her life had turned upside down and it was all Christian's fault, due to his selfish ways and foolish decisions regarding his business.

He'd failed his wife.

He'd failed his family.

But he knew he wasn't walking away from being "The Connect".

And he knew he was in too deep with Asia to leave her, it just wasn't happening.

"What happened to us, huh Chrissy? What did I do to you?" she asked.

His mind scanned their memories together; their lovemaking, their vows, vacations, children being born, dealing with his father's death, her miscarriage, celebrating their accomplishments. Damn, their journey together was impeccable. What happened to them? Why was he hurting her? He kept asking himself that; for four years, he asked himself why he was cheating on his beautiful black Queen.

He went back to their one year anniversary and how he'd always tell her she had him wrapped around her finger when they first met. *Man, I thought and still think Farren is the hottest woman I have ever had in my company,* he said in his mind.

"*Close your eyes…watch your step babe.*" *I held her hand, and made sure she didn't skip a step and stumble.*

"*Where are we? I have been blindfolded forever and I'm thirsty,*" *she complained.*

"*Girl come on and hush…one more step,*" *I told her. I signaled to the attendant to close the door.*

I then removed the blindfold from her eyes. "*Oh my God! Where are we, where are we going?*" *she asked. She smiled and hugged me.* "*Buckle up, we're going to Paris. Happy anniversary baby, I love you,*" *I kissed her lips. Tears instantly filled her eyes.* "*I'm so grateful for you,*" *she said her favorite words.*

She told me thank you a million times before she finally sat in her seat and buckled up.

"*Whose plane is this?*" *she asked, once we were safely in air.*

"*A friend, relax baby,*" *I said, rubbing her thigh.*

"*I'm horny,*" *she whispered in my ear.*

"*Shit me too, let's go to the bathroom.*" *I unbuckled my seatbelt and put the book I was reading on the table opposite of me.*

She unbuckled her seatbelt as well. "It's just on here. Why must we be cramped in the bathroom? Sit down," she commanded.

That was just like Farren, wanting some of this golden dick whenever and wherever she could get it. She pulled my penis out of my pants, and kissed it while looking up at me, flashing her million dollar smile. Her hazel eyes held a glimmer of hope in them…hope that we would be together forever and ever, and even after that in Heaven we would be together.

"Happy Anniversary, baby," she told me, before lowering her head and allowing every single inch of my dick to go down her wet and hot throat.

Farren's mouth was always piping hot; her mouth was so tight that it felt like a virgin's pussy. I loved the way she sucked my dick and was never able to last long when she had her lips wrapped around HIM. HE had a mind of his own, and Farren was his master. She used her tongue to bring me to life. With the other hand, she found her way inside of my slacks and massaged my balls. After gathering enough spit in her mouth, she spit all over my dick, making sure to not make a mess. She licked it up before it could spill, using her tongue skills to make it nasty. She began to suck and gag at the same damn time.

Eyes rolling, toes curling, biting the inside of my lip, and calling for my mama, I released into her mouth as we changed time zones.

"Come sit on your dick." I helped her up and kissed her in the mouth, before forcing her to ride me as smooth as our flight was.

"Slow.....baby...slow." Farren was bucking like an equestrian, but I was high and tipsy; I wanted this to be slow and sticky.

"Hmm....." she moaned quietly. I leaned her back and her head rested in the crook of my neck. I nibbled on her ear while whispering sweet nothings.

"You know you're mines forever, don't you?" She nodded and bit her lip.

"I love you more than anything in this world, baby."

"It's me and you against the world"

"I'ma make you my wife soon."

She was taking all this dick, and baby was going to get anything she set her eyes on once we touched down in Paris.

Farren was different; she was in a category all of her own. No one could ever come between what we built. We built our foundation off of friendship first then love. That's why we were so solid.

Fifteen years later, their one year anniversary still remained Christian's favorite anniversary out of all of them. Farren was young and in her prime back then. She laughed and smiled at everything he did. Standing before this angry woman, he almost didn't recognize her; this wasn't his sweet Farren.

"I love you so much. Let's lay down." He led her to the bed, yet she never bothered to wipe her tears.

"Since when did you ignore my questions? You keep ignoring me," she said, her voice was weak. It pained him to not hear her speak with confidence.

"Farren baby, please go to sleep." He was damn near begging at this point. She huffed and puffed while he went to shower. He took a quick shower. He didn't want to face his fears or deal with his infidelity. He knew he was fuckin up; his daddy would be so disappointed in him right now. When he entered the room they shared, she had cried herself to sleep. Her eyes were swollen and face was puffy. He slid the comforter over her body and kissed her cheek. Asking God to send him a sign on what to do and what direction to take, he joined his wife in bed.

Christian woke up to breakfast being cooked, which was normal in their home. Farren cooked two or three times a day and still managed to be the top attorney in Philadelphia. She was a woman that wore many hats.

"Daddy, mommy said you not going nowhere today, you gon be with us all day so come and eat," Noel came in there tossing her neck.

"Come here, grown little girl," he tickled and kissed his youngest daughter.

"Your teeth aren't brushed!" She squirmed away and ran back to the kitchen screaming, "Daddy is up!"

Farren knew what the hell she was doing, but he would play by her rules today. It was Sunday, and he needed to spend today with the family anyway. But first thing in the morning, he was doing 120 to Asia's house.

He brushed his teeth and threw on a hoodie over his Polo pajama pants before joining his family in the breakfast area.

"Kids, go get ready for church, we cannot be late," Farren fussed as she washed dishes and brought the kitchen back to life.

"Y'all going to church?" Christian asked, shocked. They only went to church for funerals and weddings.

"You mean, WE, are going to church. Your suit is hanging up. The family is wearing coral and grey today, and we're going to take family pictures before dinner at your mother's house." She patted my shoulder before returning to our bedroom to get ready.

At church, how ironic the pastor preached on "Not Giving Up" and Farren may as well have stood up the entire service. She clapped and called on Jesus more than a few times.

They went and took pictures at some studio where her friend owed her a favor. "Y'all are one beautiful family, I must say," Christian's mother said over Sunday dinner. Farren was passing her cell phone around.

She beamed at the compliment. "Thank you Mrs. Knight."

Christian felt his phone vibrating. After pulling it out of his pocket and seeing it was Asia, he excused himself.

"This is Greg, I'll be right back."

He took the steps two at a time to get to the basement in his mother's home.

"Can you talk?" she asked, once he said hello.

"Why didn't you tell me the Feds talked to you?" he asked. She said nothing. "We can't talk about that over the..."

"I'm not worried about them fuckers. What's up? When were you going to tell me?"

"Whoa, I don't like how you're talking to me."

"Can I trust you?" he asked.

"Really Chrissy!" she screamed.

"I'm dead ass serious Asia," he yelled back.

"Fuck you don't ever question my loyalty," she said and hung the phone up.

He called her back three more times before giving up. He knew he had been gone too long.

As he was walking back up the steps, he saw Farren standing at the top. "Can you trust her?" she asked and walked off.

He got back to the dining room to see Greg stuffing his face. "Christian I thought you said Greg called you?" his sister Chloe asked.

"I said Garett, you listening too hard sis. Wasup man" he dapped his best friend up. Courtney and Farren both shook their head at Christian's careless lie.

Farren

I had become pitiful. I turned into the woman I never wanted to be: desperate. Never had I been weak in my marriage, or emotional. I knew my husband was coming home every night and he was coming home to tell me about his day, play with the kids and have a glass of wine with me. My life did a complete one eighty in a matter of one week, and I was confused. I didn't care that he cheated; I cared because he fell in love. It was obvious. I brought her name up every day. Even after I promised myself I wouldn't the night before, I still did. Day in and day out I brought her name up, and every time I called her a little slut bitch, I could see his spirit cringing. He didn't like the disrespect. That alone told me that he loved her, he cherished her, he respected her. My only question was did he love her more than me?

Did he lay up with her at night and promise her that he would be leaving me soon? Christian must have forgotten I played the "side line" position for years. I knew what these sorry ass niggas promised, to keep you from fussing and fighting; a couple of hundred dollars here and there to shut you up.

I wondered if this was my karma for fucking a married man and falling in love. Dice was my everything.

"Why do you have to leave? Can you just stay this one night? I promise I won't ask you ever again. I don't want to be alone tonight," I begged him once more to stay.

Dice had me put me in this nice ass condo, only to stop by, fuck me and get a good meal every now and then. I wanted more and he had been promising me more, but I have yet to see results.

We laid in our sex. An hour before, he had me in every position imaginable. I was still basking in the goodness of it.

He rubbed my back as I lay facing the opposite direction of him.

"I wish I could baby, you know I want to," he said, feeding me bullshit.

"Dice, I never ask you for anything," I whined.

"Since when?" he laughed.

"I want to wake up to you"

"I'll stay until you fall asleep, I promise." He reached over and kissed my neck, but I moved from his touch.

"Just go, don't even bother. Thanks for the dick," I brushed him off. He smacked his lips, found his clothing all over the house and got dressed. I heard him enter my bedroom again and his footsteps got closer. Dice kneeled before me and kissed my forehead. "I love you, you know that. It's not going to be always be like this, babe, I promise you…a few more months".

I stopped believing him a long time ago. I hated how much I loved him and how I felt like I couldn't be without him. I hated that about me. I used to ask God to make something happen to him just so I could be forced to move on.

I knew if it was up to me I would never walk away; I was too comfortable.

I ended my pity party as soon as my assistant told me my next appointment was on her way back.

I straightened out my dress and stood. "Hi, Robin, it's such a pleasure to finally meet you." I offered her a warm smile and handshake.

"Girl, give me a hug. I feel like you're my long lost friend," Robin hugged me. She surprised me. I was only affectionate towards my husband and children, oh, and my best friend Ashley. I didn't grow up hugging, kissing or even saying, "I love you", which is why I made it crucial that my kids knew how much I loved them. I spent more time with my daughters than anyone. Every Saturday we were together doing something fun or cultural. My daughters would know how they were to be treated when it was time for them to date and take someone serious.

"So how have you been?" she asked, once we were comfortably sitting on my couch.

I wanted to scream and shout from the top of my lungs, "I'M FUCKING MISERABLE" but yet I said, "I have been great. My cases are on the up and up, and now I'm looking into developing my brand as a black woman," I told Robin.

Robin was my lifestyle coach. Although my passion was for law, there were other areas I wanted to branch out in and win. I wanted to write a book, open up a non-profit and a boutique for the women of ages 35 and up. Robin was responsible for developing and separating Farren Knight, Attorney at Law, mother and wife to Farren Knight, a future household name.

"How are the kids?" she asked.

"They are fantastic. It's taco night at the house. So as soon as I leave here, I'm headed to the grocery store," I told her.

"And how is that handsome husband of yours?" she asked. I knew she was just warming me up, but bitch please let's get down to business. I didn't want to talk about my lying, cheating ass husband.

"He's well, we all are well. So what's the first step in creating Farren knight?" I took out my notepad.

"Well, first we want you to be relatable, so we need to know about your family and childhood. We want people to be able to connect to you. What's your relationship like with your mother?" she asked.

And I was sure my face told it all. I can't even recall the last time I had spoken with my mother honestly, and as bad as it may sound, I didn't feel bad at all. I grew up in a home where I didn't feel love or respect. My sister tormented me but I was the oldest, and my mother treated me like I was a pawn in a chess game.

I remember being a little girl, and she would make me call my daddy and beg for money; money I didn't need because he made sure I had everything I ever wanted. I used to mark an "X" on the calendar to count down the days of me going to California for the summer. His new wife loved me; she was young and cool as hell. I would return home with tons of new clothes and shoes. I remember one summer I returned home with perfume...

"Farren, what's this?" my sister asked, holding my very expensive bottle of perfume in her dirty hands.

"Give that back, my daddy bought me that," I fussed and took it out her hand.

"What is it though, and why is it in this ugly bottle?" She took it out my hand again and stared at the bottle.

"It's perfume. You spray it on to smell good," I told her.

Minutes later, I heard Neeki asking my mama if she made an 'A' on her spelling test, could she get some smell goods.

"Girl if you don't get out my damn face, I ain't got no money for no smell goods. You better put some of that baby oil on," she fussed.

"I don't wanna smell like fried chicken and cigarettes. Farren walking around here smelling good," Neeki pouted.

"Farren smells just like you, now shut your mouth and clean my kitchen," their mother yelled. She was watching television and Neeki was interrupting.

"No, she don't! Her daddy bought her perfume. Where my daddy at? I want some perfume," she asked, close to tears.

Nakia got up from their tattered couch, and barged into my room. "I asked your lil' lying ass what all your daddy bought you and you said nothing but them lil' ugly bourgeois clothes. Why did you lie?" She snatched me out of the bed and held my face tightly in her hands.

She frightened me to the point where I had peed in my pants. I was never relaxed at my house; I hated living there.

"I....I forgot mama, I'm sorry," I stuttered to get the lie out. In truth, my daddy bought me tons of stuff, but they wouldn't know that. I had my stepmother ship the majority of my nice stuff to Ashley's mom house. Her mom was way nicer than mine.

"You a lying lie, give me this damn perfume. Your lil' hot ass don't need no perfume." She snatched the perfume off the dresser and left the room. I hated living there. I vowed that as soon as she graduated from high school, I would never talk to them again.

"It's fair. If she needs something I do what I can." I hoped my answer would suffice.

"Fair? Okay... and what about you and your sister..." she scanned her notes looking for her name.

"Nikita...umm, it's fair as well," I told her.

"Are you okay?" Robin asked.

"Yes, I'm good, let's continue."

"Okay, great, how do you think your past experiences have shaped you into the woman you are now?"

Farren thought to herself, *damn what's with these questions today.* She thought back to the person she was in middle school and high school to present day. Farren came from nothing literally; she grew up in one of the toughest projects in Philadelphia. She has seen it all, done it all, been through it all.

"I came from the gutter, I'm grateful for every little thing that I have. I didn't get a cell phone that my mother wouldn't take until I was seventeen years old. I mean...I struggled; I don't hide that from anyone. But God has blessed me in a mighty way," she smiled.

"And...gutter? For those that don't know. What does gutter mean?" Robin asked.

"Food stamps, public housing, babies having babies, murders right in front of your doorstep, I have seen it all. But it made me who I am today"

"If you could describe your childhood in three words, which three words would you use?"

Farren bit her finger and removed her glasses. She twirled her wedding ringer, something she did when she was nervous. "I would use the words, hard, hard, and hard".

"No other adjectives, Mrs. Knight?" she questioned.

"Have you ever been locked in a cage?" Farren asked.

"I have not."

"It will kill you if you let it." Farren touched her knee and looked in her eyes so she could see that she was dead ass serious.

"You missed my race." Farren came out of her room in a sports bra and red shorts with socks.

Her mother had company but Farren didn't give a damn. It was her last semester in high school and her mother never supported anything she did, but she promised she would be at, at least one of her races before the season came to an end.

"What lil girl?" Nakia asked her daughter. She didn't feel like cursing out Farren's stupid ass in front of her new man.

"YOU MISSED MY RACE," she raised her voice. Neeki was in the kitchen making her a plate. After hearing Farren's voice raise, she tuned in her ears.

"Farren, if you don't get out my face I'ma knock your yellow ass out," s she clenched her teeth.

"Hit me I want you to," she pumped her chest out. Farren was fed up with the lack of support. She was mad at her mama and Dice; he didn't show up either.

"Bitch who you talking to?" Her mother raised her hand and Farren didn't flinch.

Tonight was going to be the night she beat her mama ass. She already knew it.

"I said hit me, so I can have an excuse when I drag your ass down that hallway," Farren clapped her hands.

Nikita heard the urgency in her sister's voice and she came out the kitchen. "Mama got company Farren, go to your room," she said, trying her hardest to diffuse the situation.

"I don't care. He ain't paying no bills in here. I am, with my allowance," she faced her sister and told her. Wrong decision. Her mother snuffed her, fighting dirty. Farren held her jaw, and before she could even count to three to calm down, she slapped the shit out of her mother. "That's the last time you gon put your hands on me and I mean that. I'ma start beating your ass back," Farren yelled.

Her mother grabbed her and threw her on the floor. The man who she was entertaining prior to, just stood and watched the catfight. Farren was trying to scratch her mother's eyes outs. Nikita didn't know what to do. She went to call Dice from Farren's phone.

"Babe, I know you mad at me…." he started.

"Dice, Farren fighting my mama, I don't know what to do. I can't call the police; my mama got drugs in here," she rambled.

"Hey girl, get off the phone talking crazy, I'm on the way." He disconnected the call and made an illegal U-turn in the street, headed to Hardy Projects.

He didn't feel bad for Ms. Nakia; she deserved it. Farren had been taking a lot of shit from her lately. He parked right in front of her building and jogged up the steps to the third floor, and banged on the door. Nikita opened it quickly, with tears in her eyes. It was blood on the floor and Farren was now on top of her mama, choking her and calling her ever dirty bitch in the book.

"Aye ma, chill, get off your mother babe." He attempted to pull her up, but Farren wasn't budging.

She blacked out. "GET THE FUCK OFF ME DICE, I'M NOT DONE WITH THIS BITCH," she flagged her arms in the air.

"Farren, I'ma slap the shit out of you if you hit me. Chill out. You got too much going on to be acting crazy" Dice yelled.

She caught her breath and wiped the dripping blood from her nose. Nikita helped her mother up, and once she was on her feet, she slapped her too. "You gon let her beat on me?" she cried. Dice looked over at Farren's mama, and damn her face was fucked up.

Farren smiled at her handiwork. Baby she was from Hardy; her hands were lethal.

"Dice you wanna play captain save a hoe, get her up out of here," Ms. Nakia, said limping to her room and slamming the door.

The man went after her while Nikita stood there crying.

"Come on Laila Ali. Go pack a bag and hurry up," Dice told her.

Once they were in his car, he said, "I'ma take you to a room to cool off for a couple of days. What happened?" he asked.

"Why wasn't you at my track meet?" she yelled at him.

"Aye, don't get in my car with all that yelling. I ain't your mama, I'll knock your lil' ass out," he fussed and lit a cigarette.

She looked at him with tears in her eyes. "Dice, I don't ask you to do nothing, nothing at all and you couldn't take one hour out of your day to come to my track meet?" she asked.

"I'm sorry boo, I honestly forgot. Why didn't you remind me?"

She was so through with him, he had no idea. She wanted more than what he was offering.

"It's cool".

"Did you win?" he asked.

"Boy you already know the answer to that question, don't play," she punched him in the arm.

"Baby, why you beat your mama up?" he asked her laughing.

"Cus that bitch pissed me off," she told him in a nonchalant tone. Farren was growing very tired of her mother and the lack of support, but in return, all it did was fuel her ambition to go out and make something of herself. So in some weird way, she encouraged her mother's selfish and evil ways. She knew she would never be that type of mother.

Farren was brought back to reality, with the ringing of her phone; she saw that it was the federal agents. "Why do they keep calling me?" she said aloud.

"Who?" Robin asked.

"Nobody, Robin. I'm sorry I need to reschedule." Farren stood to her feet and went to gather her things at her desk to leave.

She wasn't focused at all today, and she hated when she was knocked off her square.

"Okay, I'll get with your assistant to schedule something for next week. Farren?" she stopped at the door.

"YES?" Farren responded, clearly annoyed and in a rush to leave.

"Whatever is bothering you or has your mind boggled, let it go. I'll be in touch," Robin offered advice.

If only she knew just what Farren was going through. Once her door was closed, she returned the call.

"Farren Knight, attorney at law."

"Mrs. Knight, do you have any information for us?" the agent asked, cutting straight to the point.

"I'm unaware of what you're talking about, but I can give you my attorney's number and you can talk to him," she told the man

Click.

The line disconnected. She shrugged the shoulders, "Oh well".

Farren knew she needed to take this situation more serious, she just hoped it wasn't too late to fix it. Maybe tomorrow she would think more on it, but as of right now she just wanted to go home and cry.

She was in a bad mood and she barely ate anymore.

Love hurt. Whoever said it didn't, they lied.

Farren switched from her heels to her flats, after unplugging her cell phone and throwing everything back into her work bag. She prepared to go home.

She scanned over a picture of her and Christian on the day she graduated from law school. He was happier than she was. She missed days like these, where no one else mattered but the two of them. They would lock themselves in the house for days, no cell phones or television, just lying in bed naked and talking about their future together.

"How many kids do you want?" he asked her.

"However many you want?"

"No baby, tell me for real," he pouted. She loved when he submitted to her. "I really want five.... I want a big family, Chrissy." He saw the glimmer in her eyes when she spoke about their future.

He knew she was the one when he first met her, but Farren wasn't playing any games; she never did with him. She didn't tolerate bullshit or mediocre. She expected a lot from him and never allowed him to get lazy. She would tell him all the time, you started off opening doors and sending me roses every week, why stop now? Her standards were high and with him, they were even higher.

"Why are you so beautiful?" he asked.

"Uh...nigga I don't know, what kind of question is that? You want me to be ugly?" she scrunched her nose up. They were sitting in the living room in the dark, with only one candle illuminating the room. Christian was enjoying a Cuban cigar and Farren was taking shots by herself. He wore silk boxers, and she had on a lavender bra and thong from La Perla, with her hair flopped over her face.

"Girl hush," he told her.

"Christian did you like me for real when we first met?" she asked.

He shook his head at her. "You are fucked up right now baby"

She giggled and snorted, "No I am not!"

"Come take a shot with me." She crawled to him with a shot glass in her hand full of tequila.

He fanned her away. "You know I only drink brown."

Christian's phone rung and he ignored it. Farren noticed that he frowned up his face at the screen, but she didn't say anything; she was just happy he was in the house with her on a Saturday night.

"Don't be a bore. Come on, come on." She put the glass in his face and he pushed her hand away.

"Move man," he told her again.

She made herself comfortable in between his legs and tossed the shot back, the tequila dripping down her lips.

She used her long pink tongue to wipe it up, staring at Christian as she did the motion and he matched her intense stare.

"You so sexy to me, Farren," he whispered and put the cigar out.

She took her time taking his dick out of his boxers, before licking her lips and tasting her man. They had been spending so much time together. She knew she this was who she would spend the rest of her life with; she felt it in her spirit.

It was how he was concerned with her well-being, the way he held her hand when they said grace and prayed for better days, how he brought her lunch because she was too lazy to leave the house; she was attentive and she listened more than she spoke. She trusted him and let him lead.

"I LOVE YOU CHRISTIAN," she mumbled with his dick down her throat.

He slid down on the couch to get comfortable and allowed Farren to suck the stress out of him.

He grabbed a fistful of her hair. When Farren didn't move his hand he knew she was drunk, because normally she didn't like her head to be touched. He got comfortable and started bobbing her head in a way that he liked. She must have enjoyed it as well, because he saw her sneak her finger in between her legs, and instantly he got jealous.

He was the only person who belonged in between her legs, not even Farren could touch herself and technically, that was her pussy. Christian really was crazy; he really believed her pussy was all his.

"Farren....baby" he pulled her head up from his dick; the sound her lips made caused cum to ooze out of his dick.

"Shit" he yelled, knowing his girl wasn't done with him. Farren used her other hand to squeeze every ounce of whiteness out of him and she licked every drop, making sure he was as clean as he was before they started getting nasty.

He moved out of her reach, and flipped her over diving head first into her pussy. He was so thirsty to taste her he didn't even bother taking the panties off, he just slid them to the side. She was drunk as hell, so the pussy was dripping like a broken water fountain; it was fat and swollen, and he wondered for a second was she pregnant.

"Hmmm, yes daddy, eat your pussy," she edged him on. Farren always pepped Christian up during sex and foreplay. When she told him he was beating her pussy up and eating her soul out, she meant every single word she moaned and mumbled out.

Her man was the truth in bed, on the floor, in the movies, in the bathroom at work, in the shower, and in the kitchen. No matter where they were, Christian never failed to satisfy.

He flexes his muscles as he placed her legs on his shoulders. "Your pussy tastes so good," he said, sticking his face in it further. He wished his tongue was longer; he wanted Farren to really FEEL him. His tongue vibrated inside of her and right when she thought he was finishing up, he snaked his tongue faster and sucked the 'C' out of Clit.

She panted and squirmed, begging to be let go. After releasing in his mouth for the second time, he decided that he had punished her enough.

He wiped his face and made her kiss him. "Give me a kiss."

She smiled and wiped the sweat from her forehead, and kissed him in his mouth.

"I want some pussy," he told her.

"okay, give me a minute, I'm tired," she huffed and puffed.

"Mrs. Knight...Mrs. Knight..." Dolly yelled her boss' name. Farren had her legs propped up on her desk, wide open; she looked to be in a daze. Dolly had been really worried her, but was scared to say something.

"Huh? What time is it? I have to go," she hopped up and pulled her keys out.

"Are you okay?" Dolly asked.

"Yeah I'm good. Email me if you need me."

Farren went home, but sat in her garage trying to get it together before she walked in the house. She knew she looked miserable; she'd cried the whole way home. Christian had texted her and said he picked the kids up from after school.

"Get it together girl," she told herself before she turned the doorknob to enter her house.

The house was quiet and she was worried. Normally about three televisions were on and Noel had dolls all over the house.

Farren checked the living room and saw Carren cuddled up under a blanket. She figured she had a long day at school. She went to her bedroom and saw Christian and Noel knocked out. She stood in front of him while he slept, wondering if she choked his ass could she get away with it.

Christian must have felt her standing before him. She stood there for at least fifteen minutes.

"Something is wrong with you?" he yawned.

"You're what's wrong with me," she yelled.

"Noel is sleep, lower your voice." He pulled the covers back and went to the bathroom to relieve himself.

She followed him to the bathroom. "Those agents called me again today."

"Just keep ignoring them; I'm handling the situation."

"Okay and what does that mean'?

"Since when did you start questioning me? I said it's handled," he looked at her.

"I'm about to get dinner started. I was thinking we could watch a movie afterwards."

He shook his head, "don't wait up for me," and began to get dressed.

"What you mean? I just got home, you're about to leave?"

"Yeah, you on ten right now and I got stuff to handle"

"Christian, don't do this."

"Don't do this? Why are you being so dramatic?"

"I'm not, I just don't want you to leave. I want us to spend some together," she said, her voice weak.

Christian didn't like this Farren... this whiney and annoying Farren.

"We spent all day together yesterday, so don't start," he told her.

"What the fuck is wrong with you? I am your wife. Two days in a row is too much for you? You're not doing me a favor, Christian"

"Cool, well I'll be back. Put me a plate in the microwave." he told her and left the room.

Farren needed to focus. She wanted to cry but she told herself she'd done enough crying today. She made herself do some work on a case she had coming up.

An hour later, the only thing she jotted down was her husband's name and their wedding date. She was too old to be so sprung, and it bothered her how much she loved him.

She didn't know what to do and she had nobody to talk to; well, no one that she trusted. She sucked it up and pressed forward. She made dinner, cleaned her home, did laundry and helped her children with their homework.

Since being kidnapped she refused to run or work out if she wasn't in the safety in her home. Working out was once a release of stress and she missed it so much. Especially now, when she was full of mixed emotions and didn't know what was going on. She attempted to do work again and she still couldn't. She tossed and turned all night and her mind refused to shut down.

Christian came in around three in the morning. She heard him moving around the kitchen, probably looking for his plate. She found her way in the kitchen staring at him behind a wall; he was so attractive to her.

"Farren, where is my plate?" he asked, never turning around to face her.

"I didn't make you one," she whispered.

He turned around. "It's taco night, and you didn't make me a plate?" He actually looked mad.

"No I didn't. It's taco night for a reason; a family that eats together stays together," she told him and went back to their bedroom.

It felt good to tell his ass off. She went to bed with a smile on her face, and for the first time in a few days, without crying.

Christian

I know I was wrong for how I was treating my wife. I felt my heart breaking...kind of. I'm hurting just like she is...kind of. I can't sleep at night either...actually I been sleeping pretty good. I just prayed before I closed my eyes that her crazy ass didn't kill me in my sleep.

A very small part of me wanted her to leave me so I wouldn't feel bad, but then another part of me was waiting on me to get my shit together and climb out of Asia's pussy and run back to my family. But I couldn't blame it on Asia's sex or the perfect way she rolled my blunts; we were more than that.

On the other hand, what did my wife do to deserve the harsh treatment and cold shoulder? Not a damn thing. I know karma was coming to my ass real soon.

I saw that Alonso had called me. I had an issue to resolve and he would have to wait.

I double parked in front of the nail salon that I knew Asia was at, and called her phone. "Come outside," I said, and hung the phone up. Minutes later she graced my presence, and I had to remind myself I needed to choke her ass out for keeping secrets from me. She was fanning her fingers. "Babe my nails not dry, why couldn't you wait 'til I got to the house? I told you I was coming straight there," she said, leaning on the door.

"Asia, why didn't you tell me those folks came to your door?" I asked. She smacked her lips and had the nerve to roll her eyes. "Again? Stop asking me that. I told you I didn't think nothing of it."

I banged my hand on the steering wheel. "That's bullshit and you know it. You didn't think federal agents coming to where we lay our heads were a big deal? Come on ma, don't play me like no sucker." My eyes met hers and I needed her to see the devil in them.

As cool as she was, I would swipe her fuckin head off her body if I found out she was the weak link. I worked too hard to let my sink ship because of a talking ass broad.

She looked right back at me and I could have sworn I saw the devil in her eyes, too; shit, it almost scared me.

"And I told you to stop asking me that question. I'll get up with you later" she said and walked off.

I didn't like how she was acting at all. I got out the car and grabbed her by the neck, turning her around. "I won't let you or anybody else bring me and my family down."

I had never seen her cry, not in the four years we'd been talking. "You really gon talk to me like that? You gon threaten me? After all I've done for you?" she pointed her finger at my chest.

"Your family? What about me? What the fuck do I mean to you?" she yelled.

Cars slowed down to be nosy and I wasn't feeling the attention, but I couldn't back down from her.

"I kept it real with you from the beginning, don't ever forget that," I told her, got in my truck and pulled off.

Before I could get to the next stop light, Asia had texted me.

Asia: don't bother calling or texting me because your ass is BLOCKED.

I didn't bother to text back until I got to the bottom of this open case; I didn't care whether I was blocked or not.

Alonso had called again. *Damn, what the fuck does he want*, I thought to myself

 I had too much going on and I was stressing like crazy.

"Hello?" I called him back.

"Dad wants you to fly out," he said.

"I'll be there Friday."

"Now," he instructed and hung the phone up.

FUCK! I didn't feel like dealing with this right now. I would be going on a vacation real soon, I just didn't know with whom. Farren was bitching and Asia had me blocked.

I called my wife's phone. "Yes?" she answered.

"I'm headed out of town...just wanted to let you know."

"You've been going out of town and I didn't want to know so why are you telling me now?" she asked.

Farren knew way more than I thought she knew and that wasn't sitting well with me either. Every other day she was dropping seeds in my lap.

"Like I said, I'm headed out of town and I'll be back before dinner. What you cooking?" I asked. I loved my wife's cooking.

"I'll leave your plate in the microwave," she mumbled and hung the phone up.

I would say she was crazy and tripping, but this was Farren; she was crazy when I met her.

Approximately an hour and forty minutes later, the small plane was landing on the sand in Alonso's background and I wondered was Mr. Bianchi already here.

Alonso had been a pain in my ass lately and I would ask to speak Mr. Bianchi in private if he got on my nerves tonight.

"Open your legs," a guard told me as soon as I stepped off the plane.

"I'm clean," I told him. I laid low in my city; no one knew who I was so I didn't have a reason to carry a gun.

"Christian, you must really trust me to come here without a gun. He's good, leave him alone," Mr. Bianchi said from the balcony of the house. He had a big fat cigar hanging from the side of his mouth, and he looked to be in a good mood.

Christian wasn't scared of him, but the way shit had been going lately, he would never just relax and be comfortable again until this rat was taken care of.

"You know this is my second home," I threw my hands up and smiled.

"Send him up," he told the guards.

I saw Alonso in the living room, playing the game. I was happy he was letting real bosses talk in private.

"Christian Knight, my number one supplier and biggest headache, how are you?" he patted my back and signaled for me to take a seat.

"Move away with the guns, would you? We're good, we're good," the plug fanned all of his security guards away. These niggas were strapped and trained to shoot.

They were hesitant to leave us up there to talk, but they know that Mr. Bianchi didn't repeat himself.

"Christian, I want to tell you a story," he stated.

"I'm listening."

"You remind me a lot of one of my favorite people. You know I'm not a big fan of you niggers, well he was a mixed breed, but still, he was loud and flashy like y'all niggers," he continued.

My face remained stoned. As offended as I was, he would never know. It was mandatory I made it home alive. Mr. Bianchi was ruthless and would have my head sent to my doorstep with a note.

"Few years about, well I'll say about twenty years ago, this young cat, he's from your hood actually...Dice...I miss him. He made me millions of dollars for me, but Christian, guess what?"

My ears went up when I heard that name.

I haven't heard that name in so long. He was Farren's first and when she and I first met, I always felt like I was competing with that dead nigga because she loved him so much; and when he died, he literally took her soul. But I came and brought her back to life.

"What sir?" I asked, unsure of what the hell he was about to say.

"I killed him because he couldn't locate the rat." Mr. Bianchi looked me dead in my eyes and waited on a response. He actually expected a response.

"I'm handling it," I told him.

"No you are not," he laughed and shook his head.

"You have been going on with your life, as if nothing is wrong. Those agents had your wife for hours...how did that make you feel? Can you imagine life without your wife or children or that little dark bitch you bring with you?" he loosely threatened me.

"It will be handled."

"Give me a date and time," he pressured me.

"I don't want to make an empty promise."

"That's not good enough," he wagged his finger.

"You have my word or my life," I told him and stood to shake his hand.

He hesitated before shaking it, and I let myself out.

"I will keep the agents off of you as long as I can, but handle your business. Your shipments are on hold until you do," he shouted over the balcony before I once again boarded the plane.

That didn't faze me. Even if he thought it was punishment, I was rich as hell; but I knew the streets would be pissed, and so would Greg.

On the flight back, my mind raced back to Dice and all the stories I heard about him when I was coming up in the game, compared to the few stories Farren told me about him. She was very tight lipped about their relationship. She probably felt like I was judging her, but I wasn't. Her past didn't concern me; her loyalty to me was all that mattered. I headed back home. All I wanted to do was take a shower and get some rest. First thing in the morning, I was hitting the streets.

Upon entering my home, I was greeted with the smell of fresh marijuana, and I knew Farren had been dipping into my stash.

"Safe trip?" she asked.

I ignored her question and pulled out a barstool from under the breakfast bar, sitting directly across from her.

"Baby why are you smoking in the house?" I asked.

"The kids have been sleep for hours. I haven't smoked in years," she told a small lie. I knew Farren got high from time to time. I was the one that constantly left grams here and there so she would have a lil' something at the house.

"Farren, who killed Dice? Do you know for sure?"

She looked at me and shook her head. "You still don't trust me?"

"No, no, it's nothing like that. I just want to hear the story again. You said it was one person that came in. Was he shot or stabbed, choked - what happened?" I questioned

"Christian that was so long ago."

"You never forget stuff like that, so stop trying to play me and tell me what you saw."

"All I know is before I went back in the room, I saw a man standing over him. It was his best friend and I didn't understand why would he kill Dice and they were like brothers."

"Were they business partners, or was he his connect?" She put the blunt in the ashtray and took a sip of her wine.

"I think Alonso made more money than Dice did, I can't remember."

"Alonso, did you just say Alonso?"

"Yeah Zo, you know Zo? I hate that nigga," she said.

"When was the last time you seen him?"

"It's been years a lot of years. I heard he went to Dice's funeral, shedding hella tears."

"Where were you? Did he know you were there?"

"I didn't go to the funeral, I told you that a million times."

"I'm talking about at the house."

"You know what's crazy... I used to think about that all the time. I think Zo knew I was in there, I swear he did, but I'm not sure."

"Damn," I muttered. This city was so big yet so small.

"Is everything okay?" she asked, and for a minute she sounded concerned as if I had my wife back and not the crazy woman she had turned into.

"It will be. I'm about to take a shower and get in the bed," I said as I stood to my feet.

"Chrissy?" she called out my name before I could turn the corner to leave the kitchen.

"What up boo?" I asked.

"You're not going to leave me, are you?"

Speechless. Crickets. Pen dropped. Bell chimed. All of the awkward silent moments suddenly went through my mind and I hated when she asked questions that I knew she desperately needed the answers to; but at the current time, I was unsure of where we stood and if our "love" was enough to keep me here.

"I love you, Farren," I told her and headed to the shower. That's not what she wanted to hear, I knew it wasn't.

The next morning, I was out the house before the kids could even get dressed. I was on a mission. I drove past my sister's house and saw that Greg was indeed there.

Reversing my Range Rover and pulling into her driveway, I called Greg's phone before I went to knock on the door, but he didn't answer. It was six in the morning so I'm sure he was sleep; but there was business to take care of, serious business.

I was dressed in all black and ready for war.

I used the key I had to my sister's place. It was only to be used for when she tapped out from the world, something she did quite often.

The bedroom door was wide open and there they lay peacefully. Courtney was smiling in her sleep and for that I was happy. Although I felt like Greg was not the one for her, he was indeed her breath of fresh air. I just prayed one day he would make my sister his wife, and give her the desires of her heart because Courtney deserved it. She damn near lost her life and children for him.

"Yo, my man....Greg, get up." He snored so loud I don't even see how Courtney was sleeping through this shit. But they say when you love somebody you turn a blind eye to their flaws and shortcomings.

Courtney woke up first. "Chrissy, what are you doing here and what time is it?"

He ignored her and shook Greg one more time. It was unsafe of him to sleep this hard. If someone was running up in here, he wouldn't even hear them.

Finally he opened his eyes and he didn't even reach for his gun. "You were slipping. I could have been anybody and Courtney would have been dead by now. Get dressed, I'll be outside." I left the room and went to sit in my trunk to enjoy my coffee and doughnut.

About thirty minutes later, Mr. Dead to the world hopped in the passenger seat. "What's up?"

"You gotta start getting sleep every night. I don't care what I got going on, I get at least eight hours of sleep every night." Christian didn't want to preach to him because he was a grown ass man, but in the field that they played in, he couldn't afford to lose his brother, or his right hand man.

"I've been trying to get to the bottom of this snitching situation. Man, I haven't been to sleep in days", he yawned.

"Well you want me to come back and get you in a few hours?" I asked.

His eyes popped back open. "Hell nah, sleep is for suckers like you. Let's ride," he joked.

"That's what I like to hear. First stop, Hardy Projects." Christian pulled out of the driveway and headed to the hood.

"I hate it over there, raggedy ass apartments, they need to tear them down," Greg frowned.

"Trust me, I don't like it either, but somebody knows something."

The ride was a silent one. Greg fell back asleep and Christian was tangled in his thoughts. He wanted to know who would tell and why. Did they get jammed up and had no choice? Was it a test from Mr. Bianchi, or was he the target and Christian was only a pawn in the chess game. His loyalty got him to where he is now. He respected everyone and treated the street workers to lieutenants, even the hood bitches that cooked the dope, with the same respect.

Although many of them didn't know who he was, when he did come around which was not often at all, he was cool and kind. He didn't bark orders or point the finger. He listened first before he made long-term decisions and he didn't kill on impulse or none of that young dope boy shit. Christian evaluated every situation he got himself into before coming to a concrete conclusion. He was wise beyond his years. Before he turned thirty years old, Christian had already surpassed wealth. He sat on millions of millions of dollars, yet the thrill of getting it kept him going. Christian often prayed that his greed and desire to get all he could didn't cost him his freedom.

He knew he was playing a dangerous game with the government; dangling his family's stability and security all for extra funds.

Christian knew he should have brought his "other" life to a close, but he was a risk-taker. The thrill gave him a high that no weed no matter what island it came from, could do. Being "The Connect" did something to him.

Christian and his partner Greg hopped out of the truck, making sure their guns were tucked away before walking through the infamous 'Courtyard'.

Hardy Projects was the worst neighborhood in the world, probably. So many people have lost their lives in the Courtyard; bitches fought over food stamps, men and petty issues.

Gangs came to the Courtyard to either hash their problems out or have a crazy shoot out, where multiples lives would be taken and innocent people injured.

The Courtyard constantly made the news so much to the point where even the news reporters refused to report live from Hardy Projects. They would film down the street in a lit area and have a helicopter fly over the area.

There was a myth that when the new police officers would graduate from police academy, the chief would tell the rookies on their first day, "Good Luck in the Courtyard." Police officers dreaded getting calls from Hardy Projects. Children who played in the Courtyard, parents apparently didn't care about the safety and well-being of their kids.

I would never ever allow my children to even come visit Farren's mother over here, even though they don't talk anyway. If they did, she would have to come to our house to see the kids.

"Greg, what you doing over here," a crack head asked once we made our way through the Courtyard.

Greg was the real hood star and the face of the empire; he loved the attention. Everybody fucked with Greg; all the strippers, coke boys, prostitutes, crack heads and... Everybody just loved Greg.

"Say Cornbread, what's been going over here? The Feds been coming through?"

Cornbread held his dirty finger out. Christian handed him a twenty dollar bill, waiting on the junky to drop some information on them.

"Greg who is this black ass nigga? My lips don't move for twenty dollars, shit, what he think this is," he fussed and yapped. The majority of his teeth in the bottom row were missing or rotten.

Greg pulled out three hundred dollar bills. "Man, come on with it, I ain't trying to be out here all night"

"They been out here but it's not on no snitching shit. You know Jonte back out of jail, so they just waiting on him to fuck up," he said and walked off.

"Man, you gave that raggedy ass nigga three, hundred dollar bills for that weak ass information," Christian fussed.

"Jonte, that name sounds so familiar," Greg said to himself, ignoring Christian.

"You know who Jonte is. Johan who owns all them barbershops and car washes, that's his little brother. Come on, let's go," Christian said and walked off.

He hoped the rest of the day was successful. He was more than ready to nip this shit in the bud.

Farren

"Mrs. Knight....excuse me Mrs. Knight," the judge banged his gravel to get my attention.

I was fucking up tremendously. My client snatched my arm and I almost cursed his ass out, he yanked me so rough.

"Are you okay? You're not doing good which is costing me in the long run," he said between his teeth.

"Mrs. Knight, do you need a recess?" the judge asked. He was clearly irritated.

Farren rubbed her hands together and cringed at the amount of sweat that had been produced due to her stressing.

"Mrs. Knight!" the judge said her name again.

"Sir? No sir, I apologize, I am okay." She came from behind the desk and prepared to continue the interrogation of the person sitting on the stand.

She cleared her throat and looked over her notes. "So Mr. McCauley, you're telling me that around midnight on September 9, 2012, you were at home with your wife... are you sure about that?" she asked.

"Yes, for the second time," he answered her question.

Farren thought to herself, *lying ass bastard, you probably was out fucking some lil' young girl.*

"Mrs. Knight, is that all you have?" the judge asked.

What was wrong with her today? She had to get a grip on life. She had been messing up all day in court, and this case could be huge for her career if she came out on top.

"Yes, for now, thank you your honor," she said and went back to her seat.

"The jury believes him...Mrs. Knight, what's going on?" her client asked.

"I have a headache, but we're good, don't worry," she patted his hand.

"No, you've been tripping all week. I would hate to have to get another lawyer," he threatened.

The judge banged his gravel. "Let's reschedule; be here Thursday at two o' clock. I can't take all these disruptions in my courtroom. Mrs. Knight, please be better prepared next week. Court is adjourned," he said and exited the courtroom.

"My apologies; I'll have my assistant call you tomorrow so we can schedule questioning preparation. They're definitely going to call you to the stand and we need to make sure you're ready," I told him and grabbed my leather suitcase. He saw my readiness to leave so he didn't say anything. I left and prayed that he wouldn't request a new attorney. I had been working on this case for six months and was more than qualified to represent my client; it's just I had a lot on my mind.

As soon as I got to my car, I cried. I felt like I couldn't breathe and I was losing my mind. Even my children noticed me spacing out during dinner, soccer games and extracurricular activities. I was losing my touch.

I was depressed and full of anxiety. I desperately wanted the old me back. The amount of weight I had lost in the last two weeks was ridiculous. Christian barely spoke to me or made eye contact. Every time I saw him, I wanted to ignore those pictures I saw in that interrogation room when I was abruptly taken from my neighborhood.

But whenever I closed my eyes to pray and ask God to save my marriage, I saw those pictures. I saw her smile, I saw his happiness, and I couldn't figure out when he stopped looking at me that way. No signs were obvious. I'm far from a dumb bitch. Despite my many degrees and accomplishments, I had a woman's intuition and a woman's intuition never let her down.

Christian never acted funny with me. Every now and then he would come home late, but for the most part, my husband spent his nights with me. Yeah we had a few arguments, but I couldn't recall one argument in the last few months that raised any red flags.

The only question I really needed the answer to was, "is it me?" Was I failing him as a wife or not doing my job as a mother? Was my pussy dry? That couldn't be a factor because we had mind blowing sex *every time* we touched each other. Christian could never keep his hands off of me. You know in most relationships the man starts acting funny, but he never switched up on me until now. People envied our marriage; women wished they had a man like Christian Knight. I had the total package, so why in the hell do I feel like I'm losing right now?

"NEEKI," popped up on my cell phone and I was not in the mood to talk to anyone.

Yet, I answered anyway. "Girl, what you doing tonight?" Neeki asked.

"Going home to work on this case." I really wanted to know why she called me.

"Hmm sounds boring. So girl, what your husband doing in Hardy early this morning?" she asked.

"How am I supposed to know?"

"Farren, how come every time I talk to you, you have an attitude? You need to let whatever you holding on to go. You act like you the only that grew up hard. Bitch, I lived there longer then you did and without no daddy or nigga coming to my rescue," she yelled.

One thing Farren despised more than a liar was the accuser; people who called and fussed without even asking how are you or how your day is going so far. Her sister had no idea the amount of stress she was under. Her eyes bore signs of thoughts of suicide, and her weight signified she was battling a bad case of depression.

She took a deep breath. "You don't know how I felt, you don't know what I have been through, and furthermore you can't even tell me how I'm feeling at this current moment. So you have a blessed day and please do not call me anymore. You haven't been calling, so don't start now", Farren hung the phone up.

But seconds later, her sister called back.

"Farren Knight" she answered her cell phone in the most uppity tone she could. She knew it pissed her sister off. "Just so you know, your husband don't give a fuck about you and one day real soon, mark my words Farren, you gon need somebody. Somebody that's real and won't sugarcoat shit with you, and that's your family. We are all you have, now goodbye." The line clicked.

That just might be true, who knows. Christian can walk in their house right now or better yet have the papers delivered to her office in any second, but until then, she was sticking to her husband's side like GLUE.

Farren spent the rest of the day in the dumps. She was counting down to bedtime. All she wanted to do was take a bubble bath, get drunk, and take a few Benadryl and go to sleep. She wanted to smile, but every time she tried, she couldn't think of nothing to smile about.

She cooked dinner for her family, but once again, her husband was not present at the table. She stopped making a place at the table for him weeks ago. What was the point? He never showed up anyway.

"Ma, you're not even listening to me!" Michael, her only son fussed over dinner.

"Huh, what you say baby? I'm sorry," she apologized.

"I was asking is it okay if my friends come over this weekend? I be bored," he said.

"Sure Mikey, whatever you want," she told him with a smile.

"Well can I go visit Kennedy this weekend?" Carren asked. Kennedy was in college and Carren looked up to her, but she was too young to be patrolling around a college campus.

"No, but the next time she comes to visit, I'll ask her does she want to come over and have a sleepover like the old days" Farren compromised.

No matter how long or hard her days were, she never failed to have dinner prepared for her family.

"Noel, why aren't you eating? You were my special helper today and you're not even eating the food you cooked," Farren asked her daughter.

"Where is my daddy? He never eats with us anymore," she asked and laid her head down on the table.

"Who cares, eat your food," Mike spat, and for the first time Farren read the facial expressions on her two eldest children faces; they were stale, no emotion was present. She faulted herself for a second here, wondering what the hell happened. Was she not doing a good job covering up their problems? How did the kids know what was going on? Damn Christian, she thought to herself.

"Watch your mouth," Farren scolded her kids.

"I miss my daddy," Noel started crying.

"Shut up cry baby," Carren said. She was clearly irritated.

"Come here my little baby." Farren got up, sat Noel in her lap and cradled her.

As if on cue, Mr. Christian Knight comes waltzing through the door, dressed in all black, and eyes bloodshot red.

"What's wrong with her? Hey y'all," he kissed Carren's head and dapped Michael up.

"She's too spoiled," Carren shook her head.

"And you are too so hush. Nothing, she's okay," Farren told her estranged husband. He didn't even bother kissing or hugging her, although she had barely seen him a few days.

"You never eat with us anymore," Noel turned around in her mother's lap and told her daddy who she loved so much, wiping her eyes and pouting her lips out.

Christian stood at the kitchen counter, stuffing his face with leftover pieces of chicken, and appeared visibly hurt by his youngest daughter's words. For her to be only five and even she noticed the shift in the house, Christian felt like shit.

"Daddy has been working so you can have every doll you want when Christmas comes," he told her.

"I don't want no more dolls, I want my daddy," she cried some more.

"Okay okay, calm down. Come on; let's go get ready for bed. You're just sleepy." Farren stood, cradling a crying Noel and excused the two of them from the kitchen.

"Daddy, all mama do is cry now, what's going on?" Carren asked.

Christian shook his head. "Your mama is crazy," he laughed.

But his children didn't find their mother's sudden mood change amusing at all.

"Everything is okay, I promise. Carren straighten this kitchen up for your mama, and Mike, take the trash out," he told them and went to his bedroom.

"I don't like him no more," Carren rolled her eyes and whispered to her brother. Even though she was only fourteen years old, she was no dummy. She knew her parents were having problems.

"I never did." Mike shook his head.

After getting Noel to fall asleep, Farren entered the room with her husband and she was nervous, extremely nervous. She didn't want to cause an argument with him, so she told herself to not say anything, just get in the bed and fall asleep. Maybe, just maybe, he would hold her like he used to.

Nothing happened. Farren tossed and turned all night, and Christian was sound asleep.

She sat up in the bed, and prayed for rest. But how was he able to sleep when his daughter cried for him tonight? How can someone sleep when law enforcement can come in here at any minute and take him away for years? How can you rest peacefully when your wife doesn't even look like the same woman you married fifteen years ago? It's obvious Farren was unappreciated, and he wanted to be elsewhere, but oh well. She wouldn't be leaving without a fight and all of his money.

Farren crawled out of bed and hour or two later, she found herself in their basement with a glass of red wine, wiping away tears and looking at all the letters she used to write him while she was away doing research during law school. She scanned pictures of them in Paris, Africa, Montreal, Cabo, Mexico and other places. Christian showed Farren another life. Gosh, she loved her husband something serious. It was something about him that she had never been able to put her finger on. He was just on a level all of his own. They could be in a club full of people and no matter where Farren stood, she always felt connected to her husband.

"God please save my marriage, please God. I know I have failed you, but please don't let this man leave me," she cried out with her head in her hands.

Unbeknownst to her, Carren was in the other room downstairs on the phone with some boy, and she had listened to her mother's cries and the hate began to bubble on the inside of her. She despised her father.

Carren never heard her mother cry as much as she does now. Honestly, many of Carren's friends thought that Carren's mom was mean and cold; but Carren didn't care. Farren was warm and bubbly with her and Noel. She loved her children. Farren never really shared her childhood with her children, or anyone for that matter. Christian knew bits of pieces, but she hated to go back to that dark place.

Carren didn't think her mother was cold, she just was real. She wanted to be just like her mommy when she grew up. But all of this crying had to go. At fourteen years old, she knew crying made you weak, and she didn't understand why her mother just wouldn't leave her daddy.

Farren eventually got herself together and was headed back upstairs, when she heard music playing in one of the guest bedrooms. Farren assumed it was the television that Mike probably forgot to cut off.

She entered the room and saw her daughter in there wide awake. She cut the light on and asked, "What time is it and why are you down here?"

"It's 4:42 and because I couldn't sleep," she told her mother.

"Why couldn't you sleep missy, you have school in the morning." She cut the light off and got in bed with her oldest daughter. For years, it was just her and Carren. Christian spent a lot of time out of in the streets and Farren had become very clingy to her daughter. Ever since Carren was old enough to get her fingers and toes painted, they had been going to the nail shop together.

"I don't know, ma."

"What's wrong baby?" she asked her daughter, snuggling close to her.

"Ma, why don't you leave daddy? I don't want you to be sad. You don't even look the same..." Farren cut her off.

"Watch your mouth, lower your voice and mind your business," she told her with bass in her voice, so she knew that she was very serious.

"I don't get it though, ma." She shook her head and laid down facing her mother.

"Carren, it's not for you to get, baby. I love you, and you know that your daddy loves you," she told her.

"He barely comes to anything we have at school," she fussed.

"Carren Natalia Knight! Don't you dare lay here and lie on your father."

She sat back up in the bed. "Mama, be for rcal right now. You know he doesn't come to nothing - no soccer games, recitals, nothing."

"That is not true," she rebutted.

It was then that Carren knew her father had her mother's head, and she pitied her mother.

"Okay, you're right, I'm going to sleep. Good night." She got out of the bed and left the room. Her mother was apparently going coo coo for cocoa puffs.

Farren wondered what had gotten in her daughter. She would be talking to her again, especially since she was making up lies about her father. Farren didn't like that at all.

The next morning, Farren put on the "fakest smile" she could muster up. Christian's assistant emailed her apologizing for the last minute event, but Christian's presence was requested at a luncheon the Mayor was having. Christian Knight was responsible for the majority of the new buildings that had been plastered all over downtown, so it was mandatory he was in attendance.

"What color do you want to wear?" she asked her husband, as she sat at her vanity, applying light makeup and adding her diamonds.

Farren was adjusting her three-carat diamond earrings, but they were so flashy, she decided to change into her pearls.

"I'm wearing black," he told her from his closet.

"Black? Christian it's a luncheon. Let's wear coral or yellow," she fussed.

"You can wear what you want to wear".

Counting to ten and biting her tongue, she continued brushing mascara on her eyelashes as Christian watched her from a mirror in his closet. Farren sat with her back upward; she never slouched or looked sloppy. Even in a big t-shirt and white panties, she was flawless.

"Are you going to press your hair?" he asked.

"No, I don't have time."

"You're wearing your hair curly to an event with a luncheon?"

"Look, don't come in here fucking with me. I had case prep with my client, who is two seconds away from dismissing me from this case, that I have worked my ass off on! I cancelled my work to escort you," she yelled.

"Here you go. I can't even ask you one question without you yelling, man," he threw his hands up.

"You damn right you can't, and change that tie, we are not going to a funeral; we are going to a luncheon where our colleagues will be. Black signifies death. CHANGE THAT TIE," she commanded.

Christian didn't want her any louder than she was right now, so he obeyed her and removed his black button down and traded it in for a light blue button down, grey suspenders and he added a grey blazer and a black bow tie.

When he came back out of his closet, how ironic was it that Farren had on a tiffany blue dress and grey Chanel pumps, with her hair pulled up in a neat bun. The diamonds that danced on her neck and wrist had her looking extra fresh.

"Hmmm…that should tell you something. Great minds always think alike," she told her husband. He shook his head, locked the house up and they were on their way to the luncheon.

Farren took calls the entire ride. For some reason she felt like was back on her A-Game today.

Christian wouldn't say anything, but he loved to see Farren fussing on the phone to her team. He wanted to pull the car over and give her some of this dope dick, but they had prior engagements.

"Come here, let me fix your shirt." Farren handed Christian her clutch as she made sure her husband's appearance was together. She used a little bit of spit from her mouth to get something out of his eye, and he didn't fuss.

Many people always said your wife was to represent you well, but Farren felt like it was an equal thing, especially at events like this. Everyone knew the Knight's always arrived late, dressed to impress and they never left any charity event without donating nothing less than a million dollars. Their calendar was full of events such as these.

"We're at table three, come on." Christian held his wife's hand as they went from the back of the convention center to the front. Farren kept stopping to speak to the wives. She hadn't shown up to any of the social club meetings or the spa dates they had every first Saturday of the month, for the last five years.

Farren couldn't pretend any longer, she just didn't want to. She told herself that this morning, but yet again, she was at yet another luncheon, matching her husband, and smiling as if they were the perfect couple.

The luncheon was very nice. The food was great and Christian was presented with the Humanitarian of the Year award. Farren clapped along with everyone else, as Christian went to the stage to get the award.

She yawned and Christian saw her do it from the stage. The look he gave her frightened Farren. This wasn't his first time getting this award, nor was it the second or the third. Christian donated money to every present non-profit organization. He was all for making the community safer, but yet he supplied drugs to the entire United States of America, which made her wonder for the first time did he really care about the community or was he just getting rid of all that money he acquired.

Farren shook her head of the negative thoughts about her "beloved" husband, and focused on his speech.

"First, I wouldn't be standing here before you, without my personal savior and my parents," he said.

Farren rolled her eyes. When was the last time he went to church willingly? His mother blew their phone up every Sunday morning.

"Secondly, my best friend, my prayer warrior, the hottest woman in here today, my rib and heartbeat, Mrs. Farren Knight, Attorney at Law. She's not only the mother of our three beautiful children, but she uplifts me and she does all the work; I just come up here and accept the awards." The crowd laughed at Christian's jokes.

Little did they know, he was telling the truth. I was the one that did research on real estate and prime property in Philadelphia and New York. I was the one who would be up all night, looking at ideas from the ancient Greek periods to redesign the city council's offices. I ordered paint and supplies, because his raggedy staff didn't know how.

It's crazy that none of that stuff ever bothered me until now. I didn't care before because I did it from the heart. But Christian thought he was going to leave me and still be successful? I found that funny. Yeah, he was rich before I met him, but his lifestyle wasn't damn near what it was now. It was me dragging him to events telling him he needed to befriend the Police Chief, the Headmaster of the school our children now attend, the Prime Minister and all major government officials in our city.

Christian better think long and hard before he ever muttered the words, "divorce" to me.

Snapping out of my thoughts, I noticed he was sitting back next to me, rubbing my hand. I rolled my eyes; this nigga was a movie to me.

After the luncheon came to a close, I left Christian with his friends and associates and went to find my "friends".

"Oh, no ma'am, don't come over here Ms. Hollywood," Shelbi shook her head and wagged her finger.

I laughed. "Y'all don't miss me?" I asked.

"Of course, missy, what's been up, where have you been?" Loriel asked.

I hung with the "Who's Who" of Philadelphia. They were all educated women and I wouldn't lie and say I didn't enjoy their company because I did. I just wondered If Christian left me would they disown me like they did the other women over the years. It was like your wedding ring had to be over eight carats to join their club; marriage was everything to these women.

"WORKING! You know I have that Darrian Morris case," I told the ladies.

"Geesh, be careful," Shelbi told me sincerely.

"I am. You know Christian is all over me about the case," I lied. Christian hadn't asked one question about my case.

"How are the kids?" Loriel asked.

"They're good, we are all good, just working. Let's get together soon. Christian is flashing me the 'I'm ready to go' look." I kissed all of their cheeks and went to meet my husband.

"I missed the girls," I told Christian once we were back in the car and on the highway.

"You should invite them over next week. It might cheer you up to hang with your friends," he told her.

She shook her head. "Hmm... hmm, I'll think about it"

"What are you doing today?" I asked my husband.

"Handling business." He was being so short.

"And then what? Maybe we can take the kids to the circus and then to get pizza," I suggested.

"If I'm done doing what I have to do, I'll meet y'all there."

"Christian, the kids are noticing what's going on," I told him.

"And whose fault is that, Farren? It's yours! If you stop crying in front of them, they wouldn't know," he fussed. She turned in her seat and looked at the side of his face. There was a time when he would come get her from work and Farren would ride around with him all day, running errands and sitting in on meetings. They were a TEAM.

"What the hell is wrong with you? Christian, where is this coming from?" she asked.

He ignored her and turned the radio up. Farren turned the radio down quick fast. "I'm talking to you! What did I do to you? You didn't even give me a warning or a sign. We just got back from Dubai, a week later the Feds ask me to come in for questioning, and you've been acting stupid ever since then," she continued.

"Are you trying to push me away, so if something happens to you we won't be in danger? If that's what it is then say that," she yelled.

"Farren, WE don't have to do anything with that case," he motioned with his fingers.

"You're not gon blame US on ME, I did nothing to you," she cried.

He exhaled. "Can you please stop crying. When did you start crying so much, damn," he said.

"When you stopped saying 'I love you'. Christian, we have NEVER gone this long without sex, ever," she admitted.

And it was the truth. The couple had an active and happy sex life. All Farren wanted was answers. Wow! Approximately sixty minutes ago she was happy and smiling, now her eyeliner was running down her face and she was pissed the fuck off.

"Please, tell me Christian. I can't sleep at night, I just want to know how I can fix this," she pleaded for an explanation.

"How did we get here baby? Tell me please, Chrissy, I love you," she continued.

He turned the radio up and she glimpsed over at him and saw a tear rolling down his face as well.

"What are you crying for? I'm the one that's hurting," she yelled.

He wiped his face. "Farren…. I never wanted to tell you this." He parked the car in the front of their house.

"I dare you, I mother fucking dare you," she cried and wagged her finger in his face.

"Farren, you know this has been over," he continued.

She heaved, cried, screamed and then placed her hands over her head and sung their wedding song from the top of her lungs. "One look in your eyes, and there I see just what you mean to me. Here in my heart, I believe your love is all I'll ever need. Holding you close through the night, I need you, yeah. I look in your eyes and there I see what happiness really means. The love that we shared, makes life so sweet. Together we'll always be…" she cried and sang.

Christian laid his head back on the headrest, silently crying. His heart hurt because hers did.

Farren continued, "...this pledge of love feels so right, and I need you. Here and now, I promise to love faithfully. You're all I need, here and now, I vow to be one with thee, your love is all I need".

Christian's phone suddenly rung, and it brought him out of his emotions; it was Greg.

He cleared his throat, "Yo wasup," he said.

"You good bra?" His best friend, Christian, didn't sound his best.

"Yeah what's good?"

"We have a problem. I'll meet you at Courtney spot and get in the car with you," he said and disconnected the call.

He threw his phone on the console and looked over at his wife. She wiped her tears but they seemed to never stop.

"I'm good, go handle your business," she said in a daze.

Farren got her purse and shades off the floor.

Christian didn't know what to say. He just prayed she got some sleep and didn't spend the rest of the day crying.

"I'll call you and let you know if I can make the circus or not," he told her.

She nodded and got out of the truck.

"Christian cared, he was just busy," she kept repeating to herself. Even as she washed the dishes from breakfast this morning, she kept saying, "Christian is busy, he didn't mean what he said."

Thank God she was home alone. Her children would have thought she had lost her mind, their mother walking around in a big t-shirt that was dirty shouting from the top of her lungs, "Christian loves me, Christian loves me, Christian loves me." She didn't even bother to wipe the ruined mascara and eyeliner off her face. Farren looked crazy as hell.

Farren repeated that all day, as she made her kids' beds, ironed their clothes for the next day, prepared dinner, did laundry and even reorganized her closet.

"Chrissy loves me, Chrissy loves me, Chrissy loves me," she constantly repeated.

She noticed she was out of wine and it was time for her to pick up the kids. She slid on an old pair of Timberlands, that she called her "garden shoes" because she only wore the dirty shoes when she was working in her garden. Farren headed to the local liquor store looking just like that.

"Mrs. Knight, is everything okay today?" the store clerk asked. He had NEVER seen Farren look like that. She always came in dressed for the designer Gods.

"Yes, I'm fine, keep the change." She handed him a one hundred dollar bill and went to her truck. She didn't bother waiting until she got home; she started guzzling the bottle right then and there.

Farren pulled up in the parent pick-up lane, and waited on her children to get in the car.

"Ma, what's wrong with your hair...and your face?" Carren asked, as she slid in the front seat.

"Shut up and put your seat belt on," she told her child. She didn't bother to ask her kids how their day was or did they have any homework. She turned the radio back up; she had been listening to her wedding song all day.

The kids were scared; their mom was drinking, singing loud and driving crazy, but they made it home safely.

"Dinner is on the stove. Don't be making a lot of noise or I'ma tear all y'all up," she said and went to her room, slamming the door.

Farren got high as a kite and drunk as a skunk. In between singing her wedding song, and watching home videos that her and Christian made over the years, she thought to herself, *how dare this nigga think he gon leave me.*

Her mind went back to years ago, when she found out she was pregnant again and he told her she had no choice but to get an abortion. Now it all made sense. That nigga was going to leave her all alone.

She laughed aloud, "not over my dead body."

Farren ended up passing out and before she knew it, the next day had come and left.

She woke up with a banging headache and fished around the bed for her phone. "Here, you missed court." Christian tossed the phone to her as he laid in the chaise on her side of the room, looking over documents.

"You went through my phone?" she asked.

"You ain't talking to nobody anyway, so why does it matter," he spat.

"What time is it? I gotta call the judge." She tried to sit up but the way her head was feeling, she had to lay back down.

"I talked to him. I told him Noel had a stomach bug; he owed me a favor," he told her.

"Where are the kids? Did they get to school?"

"Yeah, look, what's up? I come home and you're passed out, wine spilled all in the sheets, house smelling like weed, then you got my dick on the screen. Noel didn't know what that was," Christian scolded his wife as if she was a child.

She took a deep breath. *Damn my head hurting,* she thought to herself.

"Farren, you have to live your life for you, not for me, not even for the kids but for you," he told her.

"I have to go check on my sister. Mama thinks she done blacked out again." He stood up, kissed my forehead and left the room.

Christian failed to bring up that he was the reason I was acting this way. How do you begin to tell someone, "I can't do this anymore" and expect them to go on with their day as if you didn't say anything.

She was failing at life and she knew it. Farren silently prayed that she got it together real soon. She'd put herself through law school with nobody's help. She worked damn hard to get to where she was now, and she didn't do it sucking dick or being bent over. She worked two jobs and had loans up to her knees. Although they were now paid off, she never forgot her struggle. It humbled her and made her the strong woman she once was. She owed her children an apology for her behavior, and she knew just the way to make it up to them...if only she could get out the damn bed. After trying two more times to get up, she gave up and fell back asleep.

Christian

I faulted Greg for my sister's blackouts, I really did. Although she was a grown woman, Courtney had not been the same since she tried to kill herself and had that miscarriage.

I entered the house not knowing what to expect, but surprisingly Courtney was sitting on the couch in her pajamas watching soap operas. She'd stopped working a long, long time ago. Between me and Greg, more Greg than me, Courtney had no worries.

She spent her days couponing and gardening. I prayed my sister was genuinely happy.

"Did mama send you?" she asked, never even bothering to turn around and greet me.

"Yes she did. What's up sis, you good?" I grabbed a bottle of water from the kitchen then joined her in the living room.

"I hate talking to her sometimes. We had a normal conversation. I didn't call her crying or anything. Why did she call you?" she fussed.

"She's always worried about us. That's our mama and she ain't got no life" I laughed.

"She need to get a man and leave me alone," Courtney said, seriously.

I didn't find that funny. My father died years ago, but I would never accept another man in the house. He struggled his whole life to keep that roof over our heads.

"What you got planned today?" I asked her.

"Nothing. I haven't seen Greg in two days and he hasn't answered the phone either," she said sadly.

I bit the inside of my mouth to keep from saying what I wanted to say. "We've been real busy lately, sis," I told her, and that was the truth.

"But you went home to Farren last night didn't you? So where did he go?" she asked, checking her phone again.

"Courtney, what are y'all? You been chasing him since we were in middle school, don't you want more?" I asked. I couldn't help it at this point.

"We are us, and it's not for you to understand. You're about to leave your wife for a twenty-two year old stripper, like a dumb ass, and I don't judge you so mind your damn business, Chrissy," she yelled.

"She's twenty-four for one, and for two, I'm not leaving Farren, and as long as you have days like this sitting in the house acting like a lunatic, you are my business," I yelled back.

Fuck! I didn't mean to call her a lunatic. Courtney hated that word. That's what her kids called her when they would come to her house for the weekends. Courtney despised that word.

"Courtney, I did not mean that," I went to hug her.

"GET OUT!" she yelled.

"Sis," I tried again.

"Get the fuck out my house." She threw a beer bottle at me, and my sister did not miss. Blood trickled down from my forehead.

"Get out, get out, get out, get the fuck out my house before I call the police." This was the Courtney that I hated. She would go from zero to one hundred real quick. I left quickly, scared that if I didn't, she probably would have shot at my ass.

I pulled over at the CVS to buy some Band-Aids and alcohol. Damn, Courtney messed this sexy ass chocolate skin up. Asia called me and I sent her to voicemail. Until she had a good enough explanation for why she didn't tell me about those agents approaching her, I had nothing to say to her.

At this current moment, I didn't want to be with her sneaky self *or* Farren's drunk, dramatic ass.

Before I could start the car and pull off, an Italian man was knocking on my door with a smile plastered on his face. I didn't know if I should reach for the .40 under my seat or unlock my door. He knocked again and I decided to take the latter. I unlocked the door and he slid in.

"Mr. Knight, consider this as a countdown from the bottom to the top," he said and removed himself from the car.

I locked the door and pulled the fuck off. I feared no one. I was The Connect, don't get it twisted, but those Italians were in their own league and they didn't play fair.

I had to get out the game and fast.

I went to holler at Greg. I pulled up to his trap, rolled the window down and told one of the local crack heads to go get Greg.

Minutes later, he entered the car with a smug look on his face. "What's wrong with you?" I asked when I pulled off.

"What you say to Courtney about me? Really, I don't even care. That's your sister but that's my girl, so fall back," he shot.

"Respect," I said and left the situation there. It was too much shit going on for me to be arguing with my best friend over something so petty.

He went to stretch his legs and couldn't. "Why you ain't put your groceries in the trunk, and nigga, since when did you start doing grocery shopping? Farren done cut your ass off," he laughed.

I was too busy replying to an email sent by my accountant. "Huh? What groceries?" I asked, not looking up.

Greg ignored him. "Aye, you got some chips in this bag?" He asked, picking it up.

"Shit, what you go buy, a watermelon?" He opened the bag and almost threw up.

"Nigga, what the fuck?" Christian asked.

Greg let the window down to regain control of his breathing, as tears fell down his face. Christian continued to question him, but Greg was in a daze; he didn't even hear Christian.

Christian pulled into the Popeye's parking lot, and put the truck in park and peeped in the bag.

"Fuck," he yelled and banged his hand on his steering wheel until his knuckles bled.

In a brown, tattered grocery bag from Publix grocery store, was the head of his most loyal soldiers, Ramone. Ramone was a young nigga, but he was lethal. He had a trigger finger and didn't play when it came to Christian.

He loved when lil' Ramone came out to the clubs with him. He would hand him a thousand ones and tell him enjoy life and turn up on the haters in the club. Ramone had a promising future in the drug game. It's hard to find dedicated niggas in this life and he was definitely one of them.

"Where does his mama stay?" I asked Greg, about an hour later.

"Round the corner from your mama," he mumbled, and wiped the sweat from his forehead. It was going to be a sad day in the hood. I went to the bank and got a check for one million dollars. Although it wouldn't bring Ramone back, it was the only way I knew how to show my condolences.

We knocked on the door again, and patiently waited on his mother to come to the door. I never knew Ramone stayed so close to my hood.

"Who is it?" a cheerful voice asked behind the wooden door.

"Friends of Ramone," I said in a sad tone. Seconds later, doors unlocked and the lady stood in the store.

"Ramone doesn't live here anymore. He normally comes over on Sundays. How can I help y'all? Hey...ain't your daddy, Charles?" the old lady asked.

I nodded my head, "yes ma'am. May we come in?" I asked. She let us in and I stopped to look over the pictures of Ramone as a young boy. He had grown into a nice and respectful young man.

"How can I help y'all?" she asked.

"I'm not sure if you know it or not, but Ramone worked for us. We made sure he was taken care of and it hurts us to come here and tell you this but last night..." Greg started to tell her that her son was brutally murdered.

"Oh my Lord...I knew that boy was up to something," she held her chest and cried from her soul.

We stood to give her some time to mourn. "Ma'am, this is a check to express our sympathy for your loss; we, too, are mourning. Every year around this time, someone will drop a check in this same amount to you...do you understand what I am saying?" I asked her. I needed her to see the death in my eyes. I had no problem shooting her right between her eyes if I heard she even mumbled anything. "A young woman will come over tomorrow to go over details of what you need to say when you call the police to report your son missing. Please answer the door. We will handle all funeral arrangements as well," I continued. She took the check and nodded her head. She didn't bother seeing us to the door, so we exited quickly.

"You think she going to say something?" Greg asked, once we got in the car.

"Hell nah, that check was looking to lovely to her," I told him, and removed my black gloves. I refused to leave my prints anywhere. I wore my black gloves faithfully.

"Damn Ramone," Greg mumbled. We headed to the liquor store to rack up on Hennessy; it was going to be a long night in the hood. I had to lay low, so I would be mourning his death from the house.

"I'ma get up with you bro." I dropped Greg back off at his spot.

"You sliding through later?" he asked, after having some of the young boys get the cases of alcohol out the trunk.

"I doubt it, I gotta lay low; these folks killing left and right. I'ma lock my house down tonight," I told him.

He dapped me up. "Shit, I feel that. I'm about to go check on your sister," he said.

"Salute. Love you man, keep your eyes open," I told him, pulling off and honking the horn as I drove out the hood and headed back to the suburbs.

Asia called me again. My day was too long to be dealing with more bullshit. "Yes?" I answered the call.

She moaned into the phone, "I'm sorry," she whispered.

"What you over there doing?" It didn't hurt to go get some of that good ass pussy, to calm my nerves.

"Thinking about you," she hissed. He could only imagine what position she was in as she played in her pussy.

"I'm on the way, keep it wet," I told her and did an illegal U-turn in the middle of the street.

He left his truck with valet and used his key to enter their condo.

Christian left his shoes in the foyer, and found his lover in the kitchen eating hot Cheetos.

"Damn you just killed my fantasy," he couldn't do nothing but laugh.

"Where's the lingerie and candles?" he asked.

"Chris, fuck you, just like a nigga. Pussy make you come," she spat. Asia walked back to her bedroom, with leggings and a t-shirt on and her hair in rollers.

This is not what he did one twenty down the highway to see. "What are you talking about?" he asked her smacking her ass. He refused to leave without getting some pussy, but it looked like Asia was not in the mood.

"Get off me." She pressed play on the television. It looked like she was watching Hot Boyz.

"You just wanted to see me, huh?" I asked her, as I took my clothes off, and slid on some basketball shorts. It had been a minute since I'd been over to see her.

"Are we done or what? Let me know so I can move on," she asked.

"Girl, please," he brushed her comment off.

Christian's downfall later in life would be that he trusted easily. He was so arrogant that he felt like he was a blessing to every woman he met. He would soon realize karma was real.

"Do you even miss me?" she asked. He never heard fear in Asia's voice, but it was there; she was worried.

"Baby, come here," he told her. She was being stubborn and acted as if she didn't even hear him.

"Come here. I miss you more than you know. I've been grinding. They killed Ramone," he whispered into her ear, once she snuggled up against him.

Asia inhaled his scent and she missed every single detail about him, down to how he kept his hands in his boxers while he slept and the way his eyes sparkled every time he looked at her. She missed her man.

"Are you okay? I'm sorry to hear that baby." She was concerned as she rubbed his face.

"I'm good. It's what happens in this life. The good always die and the flaw ass niggas are ones that live," he shook his head.

"I've missed you so much," she told him, kissing his neck.

"Show me then." He made her get on top of him. Asia bent down and kissed him all over his face, licking his neck and chest.

"Slow down, I'm not going anywhere, baby," he told her. Normally, their sex was rushed, but Christian had been neglecting her lately, and Asia was important. She was also a priority and she didn't deserve that. He made it up in his mind that the rest of today would be directed to her, forgetting he promised Farren earlier he would go to the circus with the kids tonight.

Asia rode Christian as if that was their last time together. She felt like she was losing him. Christian reassured during their lovemaking, he wasn't going anywhere and they were forever. She kept moving her ear as he snaked his tongue inside of her ear, bringing her closer to his mouth. "You know this dick yours," he told her as as he guided her hips to sway how he wanted her to.

His dick was a ship and Asia was the captain. She bit her tongue and held her head back, as her eyes rolled to the back of her head and her small titties and round nipples poked out. Christian couldn't keep his hands off of her.

Asia needed this. She savored the moment, enjoying their sex every single time. Christian was a beast in bed, never failing to please her in every single way. For hours, he reassured her that what they had was real and Asia couldn't deny the fact that he made her feel better.

He never promised to leave HER, but his time spent with Asia went up and down. Asia never asked Christian questions about HER and he never discussed Farren with her.

"I told her I didn't want to be with her anymore," he told Asia, hours later. It was random; they went from talking about getting Asia a dog to his strained marriage.

"And what did she say?" she asked.

"Nothing...she burst out singing our wedding song," he told her.

"Are you for real?" Asia laughed.

Christian didn't find his wife's pain funny at all. That was his cue to leave.

"Let me gone and get up, it's three in the morning." He peeled out of bed and got dressed.

"Come lock the door."

"Use your key," she said.

"You're not giving me a kiss or a hug?" he asked.

"Chris, you're leaving because I laughed at your wife."

"Asia, it's three in the morning. I won't be home until four-thirty. I'm pretty sure she's sitting by the door waiting on me to get there," he tried to get her to understand.

"So what? I lay here every night wishing you will come see me so what's your point?" she yelled.

He shook his head. "Goodnight" he told and left the bedroom

Asia wasn't Farren. She wouldn't be crying and chasing him. If he wanted to leave, okay, cool. She got some dick so she was good.

Christian headed home. Those Italians still had him a little shaken up. He scanned his phone seeing he had tons of missed calls and text messages, people sending their love for the death of Ramone. After scrolling down some more, he realized he forgot all about the circus and dinner. Farren sent pictures of her and the kids, and he hated he missed it.

He got home and saw that all the kids were in the bed with Farren. They looked so peaceful, and Christian knew he had to make a decision soon on what would he do. He couldn't be two places at once any longer. He moved around the room quietly and went to shower. Farren looked over at the clock on the wall and saw it that it was almost five in the morning. She shook her head and asked God to fix their marriage or send her a sign to leave.

Christian woke up early the next morning, to make his infamous pancakes for the family.

"Smells good in here." Noel came in the kitchen in her Hello Kitty pajamas. Noel had an old soul. She reminded him of his mother so much.

"Go wake everybody up," he told his daughter.

"Okay daddy and I want a whole bunch of bacon," she laughed and sped off back to her mother's bedroom.

About thirty minute later, everyone emerged to the kitchen.

"Daddy you haven't made your pancakes in forever," Carren said as they sat at the table, eating.

Farren ate in silence. "What are y'all doing today?" Christian asked his family. He felt like a stranger in his own home, but he was unsure if it was his guilty conscience or not.

"Mommy said we had to do our homework before we made any plans," Noel said, stuffing her mouth with grits.

"That's right, school first," he added.

"Let me get to work." Farren stood up and went to wash the dishes.

"You going in the office on a Saturday?" he asked.

"Yeah, if I don't want to lose this case I gotta get on it," she told him, not daring to turn around. She cleaned the kitchen in silence.

"When I get back, y'all should be done with homework and chores. Carren, I want that room cleaned. Mike, the basement is not yours; get that downstairs together. Then we will decide on how we will spend our Saturday, I was thinkingggggg.....ice cream and the art museum" Farren told her kids.

"Yay!" Noel jumped up and down. Carren looked happy, too.

"I don't want to do that," Mike complained.

The girls were mini Farren's. She was cultural and appreciated the finer things of life. She and the girls were always going to different art galleries and fashion shows.

"Mike, we can go to the arcade or something today, man, what you want to do?" I asked my son.

He looked at me. "I'll just go with mama," he said and went to his room. The tension was pretty thick in the room. Farren ignored it and went to our bedroom to get dressed. I followed closely behind her. "What's going on?" I asked her.

"Excuse me?" she asked, pulling a t-shirt on over her bra.

"What's wrong with Michael?"

"That's your son, you figure out. I don't have all the answers." She pulled some tight jeans over her round ass and slid her pedicured feet into a pair of Gucci sandals. "I'll be back. If you leave, drop the kids off at your mama's house. I don't want them hear alone until that case is closed," she told me and left the room.

Christian went to talk to his son, but before he could make it up the stairs, his phone was ringing and he already knew who it was.

"Hello?" he answered on the second ring.

"Body two...tick tock," and the line clicked.

What kind of evil ass game is Mr. Bianchi playing and what the hell did he do to deserve it.

He went to his office to have a drink. Christian didn't care that it was still morning time. Bodies were dropping like flies and he didn't know how to react or what path to take to find the rat.

Christian wanted to ask the Italians so bad, if it's so easy for y'all to track me down and keep tabs on my family, friends and soldiers then why can't y'all find the rat and handle the problem. Why was he the one to blame? Christian prayed that this situation didn't get out of hand, and most importantly his family wasn't hurt in the end. He would then have to take off his million-dollar smile and replace it with the look and spirit of death. Christian never had to do much enforcement or killing because any major problems that he had, the Italians handled. This is why he was still kind of confused as to what the hell was going on. He wondered if there was was another underlying issue. Time would tell and all lies would be revealed.

Farren

"Mrs. Knight, haven't seen you in the office on a Saturday in God knows when. Are you still working on the Morris case?" the head partner of the firm where I worked, peeked his head into my office.

I was not in the mood to talk. "Yes sir, I'm the lead attorney," I said matter-of-factly.

He came in and closed the door. "Umm... Farren, when was the last time you checked your email? Morgan took the case on yesterday. She requested the files from your assistant. Has she not received them yet?" he asked.

Farren couldn't believe this shit. She worked diligently. That case was going to take her career off and she would finally receive the recognition she deserved.

She fought back tears. "No sir, I have been busy with my children. I will get those to her Monday morning." She didn't look up as she closed her laptop.

"Before Monday, this is a big case," he said and exited her office.

Was Farren that bad of an attorney? She wanted to call Mr. Morris and ask him for another chance. The work was basically laid out for Morgan, all she had to do was present it. But no one could present the work like Farren.

She blamed Christian for the case being taken away. If she wasn't kissing his ass she would have been more focused on her job.

She left the office angry. If she didn't have her career then what did she have to look forward to every day? She was a mother first, of course, but Farren enjoyed making her own money. She didn't ask Christian for anything, she never had. Farren remembered being pregnant with Carren; she went to work every day until her water broke.

There were a few things she didn't play about: her children and her career. There was a time when she would fight over Christian, but now she considered him community dick, meaning he was for everybody.

Farren sped down the highway, not caring that the rain was coming down fast and the roads were slick. Her phone rang. She would be so happy when Christian handled that case. Those agents called her every day, every two hours and it really got on her nerves.

She picked up the ringing phone from the passenger seat, and opened the attachment; it was from an unknown number. Pictures of Christian outside of a nail shop with HER, pictures of Christian leaving some building that she assumed was a condominium, zipping his pants up, pictures of HER pumping gas to a brand new Mercedes Benz. This nigga bought her a Mercedes Benz? She threw the phone in the back seat and sped home.

She didn't even know what "living" was anymore. What did she have in life? Where was her happiness? Where was her forever? She blamed Dice for these problems. If he would have just left her alone knowing he was a married man, she wouldn't be dealing with marital issues.

Farren sat in her garage and cried her eyes out. She was so tired of crying. She took a deep breath, trying to calm the devil on the inside of her, but she couldn't. He taunted her mentally.

The devil spoke - you should just die, he doesn't want you anymore.

An angel spoke- you have something to live for, yourself. Farren, you have yourself.

The devil spoke- everybody is going to talk about you.

An angel spoke- God will fill you up where you are weak.

The devil spoke- just go on and kill yourself; you're worthless. You can never keep a man.

Farren hated herself right now. She couldn't recall the last time she smiled or really had a good day. No matter how good she thought she was doing, when she came home to an empty bed, her spirit died.

If you have never experienced heartbreak before, then what Farren is experiencing is weird to you. But when a woman has given their all, remained loyal despite how her man treats her, when you chase and beg and it still doesn't work, that's heartbreak. Love hurts, but love isn't supposed to hurt. Love is supposed comfort and protect.

Love failed Farren and because her husband meant the WORLD to her, she didn't understand how she was supposed to focus and go on with life.

Farren entered her home in a daze. She hated to admit the devil had won. She was forced to deal with some real shit and that was she couldn't live without her husband. If he thought for a second he was going to leave her, she would make sure he hurt every day by dealing with the fact that he killed her; not physically but mentally. He led Farren to do the very thing she pitied other women for.

Letting yourself go because a man didn't want you, that was always stupid to her. Farren always told herself she knew she was the shit; she was confident that she was every man's dream. But now she wondered was she a sweet dream or a beautiful nightmare, because her man found love in the arms of someone else, and a stripper at that. Damn, a stripper got her man. She used her long legs and a pole to take a married man from his home. Farren wished death on the young bitch.

She threw a shot of patron back and did another.

She was about to kill herself. She was home alone and it was the perfect time. Farren knew people would shake their head at her. People would wonder why someone like her, a woman who appeared to have it all together would go and kill themselves.

Farren knew this act was selfish. Her mind went to her children, her father, and her business. It would all be for nothing if she gave up this easily.

As she tossed different pills back and mixed them with vodka, she sat at her kitchen table in a daze. If she couldn't be with Christian, she didn't want to live. Her promised her heaven then dragged her through hell.

Why do men treat women like this? You can be the epitome of class and grace then out of nowhere with no warning, they wake up and decide they don't love you anymore. How is that fair?

Tears fell down her face, and she felt like a failure. It wasn't that marriage was the key to a happy life, but it was the solution for her happiness. She adored her children, but without Christian there wouldn't be any children.

Prior to meeting her husband, she had zeroed love out; it was out of the equation for her. Farren brainwashed herself to feel like all she needed was her career.

If only she could close her eyes and go back to the day they first met, she could reconsider having that impromptu date at the Waffle House. She wouldn't have allowed him to become such a major aspect of her life.

She forced more pills down her throat. She remembered the first day Christian told her he loved her. She was so happy, but she had to act like she didn't care. Christian would say 'I love you' to her every day all day and Farren would act like it meant nothing to her. On the inside, her spirit was happy.

An hour after swallowing over a hundred different pills, she felt her heartbeat, slow down. Her eyes fluttered and she realized she was fucking tripping. She didn't even know who she should call or would call. She had no real friends who lived nearby, and her husband didn't give a fuck about her.

Robin! She didn't have much time. She felt her spirit leaving her body, or did she? Farren was drunk and high. Mixed in with the pills and stress, she was losing it.

She prayed Robin answered the phone, but she didn't. Farren had no choice but to call 911.

"911, what's your emergency?" the operator asked.

"I'm sick, come get me," Farren mumbled. She laid her head on the table and prayed that someone saved her life. Her phone vibrated and she wanted to answer it, but her vision became blurry, fingers weak, yet she struggled to slide the bar over to answer the call.

"Robin... I'm still in that cage," she slurred and cried.

"Farren? Huh, what did you say?" she asked.

"I'm in that cage...help," she said before falling out of her chair and hitting the floor head first.

Christian

I sat in my office with my head honchos; we had to find the rat. I wasn't in the mood to lose anyone else close to me. Farren's assistant was blowing my phone up and I didn't know what she wanted or why was she even calling me. Seconds later a text popped up. "It's Farren...please call back" the message read in all caps.

I instantly called back. "What's up?" I said. The crew got quiet, thinking I had information on the rat.

Dolly was crying profusely. I didn't understand shit she was saying.

"What? I can't hear you," I said.

"The ambulance is at your house. Farren is in there... she called 911 but they can't get in the gate. Please help. Her friend said Mrs. Knight kept saying she was in a cage," she yelled.

What the hell did Farren do? He thought to himself.

"I'm on the way. The code is 0508 and to get in our front door, the code is 1225," he said, not caring that he was in a room of people he thought he could trust.

"I'm on the way," he said and hung the phone up.

"Greg, ride with me man," he told his best friend. Christian put his emergency lights on and got to his house as soon as possible.

A stretcher was being lifted into an ambulance. Christian barely parked before getting out, asking what happened.

"That's my wife...hold on, that's my wife, what happened?" he asked.

"Overdose. We need to get her stomach pumped as soon as possible," the paramedic said and got in the truck.

"Overdose?" Greg asked.

Christian shook his head. "Dolly, can you call my mom and sisters. Tell them leave the kids at home with someone. Do not bring my kids up there." He couldn't believe this shit. He just prayed his wife through.

Her friend Robin was cleaning the kitchen up. "Who are you?" Christian asked.

"I'm a friend of Farren's. I've met you before at her dinner last year. She called me and said she was in a cage, I was just trying to help clean up," she rambled. She looked hurt by Farren's suicide attempt.

"Oh okay, well I'm about to lock the house up, I'll clean that up. We will be at River Oaks Hospital," I told her, and escorted her to the door.

I didn't know this lady and I didn't want her wandering around my house.

"Why would Farren want to kill herself?" Christian mother kept asking aloud. They had been at the hospital for hours waiting to hear news about Farren.

Christian sat in a corner by himself, tapping his leg, praying for the best.

"Ma, we don't know. She's been crazy if you ask me," Chloe said rolling her eyes.

"You don't even know her." Courtney hated the way her sister acted sometimes.

"Christian....Knight, family of Farren Knight?" the doctor asked.

"That's my sister, why is my sister here?" Farren's sister came out of nowhere. I looked over at her, and she was in scrubs but she still had her purse and book bag; guess she was just getting to work.

"We are here, what's the news Doc?" I asked.

"She is a fighter, I will tell you that. The amount of alcohol is affecting her liver, so I suggest she slow it down. She is now stable, and if y'all wanna see her, y'all can. And this was definitely a suicide attempt. She can't leave without a psychiatric evaluation. It's hospital policy." He signed off on a clipboard before walking off.

Christian sat back down. "You don't want to see your wife?" his mother asked.

"Y'all can go ahead," he told his family.

"You are pitiful. Get your shit together," Courtney mushed him in the head and went to see her sister-in-law. Thirty minutes later, they returned and told him they would make sure the kids were well taken care of until Farren felt better.

"You better tighten up son, and I mean it. That girl look like she wanted to die," his mother whispered in his ear and kissed his cheek.

Christian was left in the lobby to deal with his emotions and his thoughts. He didn't want to face Farren right now.

"Robin? Is that your name? You can go see Farren. I'll be back later," he told her "friend".

She looked very surprised that he didn't want to see his wife, whose life was just saved by the grace of God, but she didn't say anything; it wasn't her place.

Christian left the hospital with no destination in mind. He just drove around in circles.

Farren

"Farren?" A knock was at the door. I really didn't want anyone else to see me like this; I was so embarrassed. I ignored the knock, hoping the person would go away. I was sedated, so it wasn't hard for me to act like I was sleep.

"It's me, Robin. How are you feeling?" She pulled a wooden chair close to my bedside.

"I'm okay, just tired. How did you know I was here?" I asked her.

She looked up at me with hurt in her eyes, and for a minute I felt like this lady really cared about me. No one ever cared about me except Christian and my best friend, but she's so far away, we barely talked.

"You called me, you don't remember? You said you were in a cage and you needed help to get out." She grabbed my hand and held it.

"I'm so...embarrassed," I whispered.

Robin Jackson was someone I planned on doing business with. What the hell was I thinking calling her in my despair?

"Please keep this between us. I don't want people to know," I told her.

"Never, that's not in my character. I see you're tired. I'll come back in the morning to check on you. Do you mind if I pray with you?" she asked.

"God's not listening to me, he never does," I mumbled, tears falling out of my eyes. I can't believe I tried to kill myself. I've never been a weak woman in my life. I always made sure I was straight. My first priority was always me. When did I replace my husband's happiness before mine?

"Hush that crazy talk. Father God, I come to you thanking you for a second chance at life. God we come to you asking for repentance for the thoughts of suicide. God we know you are a just God. God, we come to you crying out for peace and happiness. God, locate Farren a source of peace. God visit her in her dreams. I rebuke the spirit of nightmares, depression, and the spirit of loneliness. God let her know that in you, all things are made whole. God, for every setback, let her know that there is a blessing with her name on it. God, keep her near you and cover her home, her children, her career, and her finances. God, the things that she so desperately tries to take a blind eye to, open her eyes, open her ears and close her mouth. Force her to see your goodness. In Jesus' name I pray, Amen," Robin prayed.

When the prayer ended, it was like I felt better instantly. If I knew God worked that fast, I would have been praying. I squeezed her hand. "Thank you so much, Robin," I whispered. My throat was very dry.

"You want some water?" She stood to bring a plastic cup to my lips. I sat up as much as my body would allow, and took large gulps of the ice water.

"Where is Christian?" I asked her.

She took a deep breath. "He left, Farren. It's not my business and I'm only on the outside looking in, but at your house, he didn't even look the least bit concerned. He was very calm. For someone whose wife was possibly on her death bed, he was calm... real calm," she told her.

"That's just Christian; he doesn't yell, doesn't cry. He probably knew I would be okay. We are fine, Robin, I promise. Thank you," I attempted to reassure her.

She got the hint and left with promises to return tomorrow. That bastard, "the least bit concerned". So even if I was on a metal table with the white cover drape over my face, would he have been concerned then?

I couldn't believe Robin's words. I buzzed the nurse and lied and said I was in pain, so she could give me something to fall asleep. I was more relaxed in my sleep than when I was up being forced to face all of my problems.

Three days later, I was released. My Doctor had the nerve to make me go see a psychiatrist before I could be discharged.

My sister was my discharge nurse. I didn't speak to her and she didn't speak to me.

I handed her the pen back after signing my forms. "You done let that stupid ass nigga drive you to suicide, really?" she asked.

"Mind your damn business," I told her and walked off. Where was Christian? I texted him and told him I was being released today.

Neeki came from around the desk and grabbed my arm. "What is going on with you? Death? Do you know how that would have made mama feel?" she asked.

"Girl, are you serious right now? Nikita, get out of my face before I get your ass fired."

Courtney came in the lobby. "Sis, you ready?" she asked. "Where is Christian?" I asked her. I didn't want to ride with my sister-in-law, I wanted my husband to come and get me. Where was Christian?

"Farren, come on. I don't know where he is, he just asked me to take you home." She escorted me to her car.

"Courtney, where is Christian?" I asked, with tears in my eyes.

"Sis, you know I love you right? I'm about to tell you this because I have a relationship with you outside of my brother." She turned the music down.

"You need to divorce him, get custody of your kids and move. You're smart, and I know you've been saving your money. Move and start over life somewhere else," she told me.

I shook my head and wiped the tears that cascaded down my face. "No Courtney, I'm fighting for my marriage. You don't understand."

"I don't understand? Come on now, Farren, who you think you talking to? I stayed with a man for TWENTY years and he was GAY. I fought long and hard for my marriage!" she cried with me.

"Gay? Derrick was gay?" I asked. Oh hell nah, I definitely wasn't expecting that.

"Yes, but please don't tell Christian," she said.

"I lost my whole life. My kids don't even call me mama, I'm that crazy bitch. But Derrick failed to tell everybody why I was cheating on his ass. It's because he wouldn't even touch me. Farren, do you know how that feels for your husband to leave the house, when your kids go to sleep, in heels? Farren, he had on heels and a wig," she said.

"I'm so sorry, Courtney. I never knew or expected it," I shook my head.

"Listen to me, I wouldn't tell you anything wrong. My brother loves you, we all know that. But his heart not with you no more. Do not chase this man. Before you lose your damn mind, let it go," she preached.

Everything she was saying was true, but she didn't know how it felt to be alone. After Dice died, I was all alone. I had no one and I became content in my singleness. Then years later, Christian came into my life and changed my world around. It was like he readjusted the stars and the moon just so we could be together. He pointed out my flaws and made me love the very things about me that I hated. Men like Christian weren't just walking around Philadelphia. I wasn't letting him go.

We pulled up at my home; it had been three days since I was last here. Instant replay went through my head, of me swallowing all those pills and drinking. I couldn't believe I did that.

"Where are the kids?" I asked.

"With Chloe. She's going to drop them off when they get out of school. Ma made dinner just put it in the oven. I'll do that for you, now." She said while going to the kitchen.

Minutes later, "sis, I'm out, love you. Call me if you need me," she shouted from the foyer.

"Okay, thank you," I told her.

I walked in my bathroom and ran me a bubble bath. I just needed to get my thoughts together. I filled the tub with bath salts and Epsom salt, and sunk down in the bubbles.

"What am I supposed to do now?" I asked myself.

I lost my case, federal agents were harassing me, my husband fell in love with a stripper, my children damn near hate their daddy, and I had no REAL friends or family. I felt so empty.

I heard the kids running through the house, and I quickly got out the tub, dried off and slid on some yoga pants and a t-shirt. My hair was soaking wet. I threw on a shower cap and went to meet my family in the kitchen.

"Farren, how are you?" Chloe asked.

"I'm well, hi my babiesssssss, I missed y'all so much." I kissed each and every one of them.

"How was your business trip, mommy?" Noel asked.

"It was long and boring. I'm so happy to be back with y'all. Go put y'all book bags up, we're going to go skating," I told the kids.

Of course, Noel was the happiest out of the three. She took off running and went to change her clothes.

"Farren, are you really okay? Because if you aren't stable enough to keep your own children, I have plenty of my room at my house," Chloe said matter-of-factly.

"Stable? Chloe, thank you for dropping them off, goodbye" I told her, and opened the front door.

"I never understood what Christian saw in you, but that's not my business," she said and left.

One day rcal soon, she was going to catch me on a bad day and I was going to give it to her when she least expected it. For years, I allowed her to talk to me any kind of way and be downright disrespectful, and I said nothing.

I went to get dressed and blow-dry my hair. The only thing I had constant in my life were my children, and I planned on spending more and more time with them, starting with today.

Christian

"You mean to tell me you haven't been home in how long, cus I don't think I heard you correctly?" my mother fussed.

"Why are you yelling, ma, why must you yell?" I asked.

"How do you stay days away from your home? You are a married man. Do you even call and check in with your wife and kids?" she scolded.

My mama was having Sunday dinner at her house, and it was the first Sunday we had been together in a while. I didn't know she was inviting Farren.

"Chrissy, why would mama not invite Farren? Since when did Farren not come to Sunday dinner" Chloe asked.

"I'm just saying, why didn't nobody tell me?" I knew my question was stupid, but I didn't want to see her.

My actions lately reflected a coward, but Farren attempting to kill herself was a desperate attempt to get me to stay or to place my thoughts of divorce on pause, and it was a serious turn-off to me. Why would you take your life for ME when you had kids and a career to live for? It was stupid to me, and it was hard for me to even look at her, so I stayed away.

"You sound stupid as hell," Greg laughed, but I didn't find anything funny.

Farren rang the doorbell. I went to open the door because no one else made a move to get the door.

"You need to get it together," my mother fussed.

I opened the door and faced my wife, my estranged wife, my crazy ass baby mama. She was still beautiful, despite stuffing her face with pills. She looked like she just walked out of heaven. Farren was dressed comfortably, in a dress and cardigan. Noel and Carren matched her while Michael wore jeans and a t-shirt.

"Hey y'all," I said. Carren ignored me and so did my son. That surprised me. I talked to them every day over the phone. Yeah I haven't been to the house, but I still called.

"Hi daddy," Noel said, and gave me a hug.

"Y'all come back here and speak to your daddy," Farren shouted.

Carren smacked her lips and ignored her mother. She went to the kitchen to greet her cousins.

Farren stood by the door. I wondered if my mama made her come because she looked as if she'd rather be anywhere else than here on this Sunday, with my family.

"What's up Christian? Did you move out or what?" she asked.

I looked at her. "Why would you try and kill yourself?" I shook my head in disgust.

"One mistake, don't point the finger," she threw the disgust back.

"Not once, when you was popping pills and getting high, did your kids cross your mind?"

"Not once, when you been laid up with that bitch all week, did your kids cross your mind, come on, what else you got? I can go all day," she rolled her eyes.

"Farren and Christian Knight, these kids are in here and we are ready to say grace and eat. Farren, you look beautiful." My mother entered the foyer where we stood. We entered the large dining room where my kids were sitting. Courtney's kids were visiting from college. Greg, Chloe, her husband and their kids and wives, and my mother sitting at the head of the table, were all in attendance.

Kennedy stood to hug Farren. "Hi auntie," she beamed. Kennedy loved Farren and even went to Spelman to eventually become a lawyer just like her aunt.

"Hi baby, I've miss you." She kissed her cheek and took a seat in between Carren and Noel.

Thirty minutes later, everyone was too busy eating to talk.

"Farren, how is the case coming along? I have been watching the news," Chloe's husband asked.

She cleared her throat. "I'm not on the case anymore, but when I go into the office tomorrow, I will find out," she said looking down at her plate.

"The biggest case of your career...wow, I'm sorry," Chloe said.

I rolled my eyes. My sister had the ability to make anyone feel like shit.

"Are you sad, mommy?" Noel asked.

"No baby, everything happens for a reason," she told her daughter.

"I'm so happy to have all my kids and grandbabies under one roof again. If it's not Thanksgiving or Christmas, I don't see all y'all together," my mother smiled.

"To family," Courtney raised her wine glass.

"To family," everyone joined in. Farren pointed her wine glass in my direction, and mouthed, "to family" to me, and there was so much pain behind her eyes that I couldn't take it away if I wanted to.

Dinner was smooth and the food was good. "Daddy, when are you coming home?" Noel asked.

"Yes Christian, when are you going home, where you live with your wife and children?" Chloe asked, with a smile on her face.

"Chloe!" Courtney fussed.

"Noel, what did I tell you about keeping family business at home," Farren popped her in the mouth three times.

"That's right, if you don't beat them they won't learn," my mother agreed.

Noel burst out in tears and fell out of her chair, crying.

"Get up and shut up" Farren yelled.

"We are about to go, she's sleepy. Thank you for dinner." She stood up and told the kids to wash their hands so they can get ready to go home.

Farren looked so embarrassed and I sat there speechless.

"Babe, make sure they get to the car safe," Courtney said to Greg.

I couldn't move; I was numb. I didn't know what the hell was going on, I really didn't.

"Do you want a divorce, is that what it is?" my mother asked me hours later, once everyone had left and we stood in the kitchen, washing the dishes.

I loved the relationship I had with my mother. She didn't sugarcoat anything and she was always there when I needed her. She just talked entirely too much, so I was always limited when I spoke with her.

"Ma, I'm just not there anymore. I love her, I got her 'til infinity, but I just want us to raise our kids together, that's it," I admitted for the first time.

"What happened, baby?" she asked, handing me a plate to dry off.

"She stopped being Farren."

"Christian, marriage never stops, you have to keep it going, growing, dating, and working on it. It doesn't fix itself," she told me.

I shook my head. Ma wasn't getting it. "That's the point, I don't want to fix it. I want to move out," I told her.

"We did not raise y'all like that and you know it. Divorce is frowned upon in the bible," she disagreed with me.

"I don't know what to do." I was frustrated and tired.

"Pray... God has all the answers you need," she patted my back and said. "Finish up the dishes, then bring me a beer."

I chuckled. My mother was old school. She wasn't going to sit up and waste her energy all day. If you didn't want to listen, then that was on you.

Things couldn't continue to go on this way. I had to make a decision on what I wanted to do and how I wanted to spend the rest of my life; but I wasn't thinking about it tonight.

I stripped down to my boxers and fell asleep in my old bed. My room was the same room I grew up in. My mother never changed anything around. She never boxed my daddy's belongings up and moved them to the attic. It was true that my daddy's presence was still felt in the house. I needed to talk to him. If only Heaven could take phone calls, I would have my daddy on speed dial.

Before I knew it, my mama was knocking on my door telling me to come eat. Shit, if me and Farren didn't work out, I could always move back home; my mama probably would love that.

"Hey ma, I'm just gon move back in here. I'ma bring some of my clothes back tonight," I told her, as she sat a full plate of pancakes, turkey sausage, cheese grits and eggs in front of me.

"Oh no sir, I done raised my kids. This is MY house," she told me.

"You know you want me to move back in. You in this house all by yourself," I told her. Mama was trying to act all hard.

"Christian, I have company over here about twice a week, so technically I am not alone. And speaking of my company, when are you leaving? I have plans today," she told me.

"Huh? Whoa! Hold on, time out. Company? Twice a week? Since when?" I felt my blood pressure rising.

"I'm grown, now eat up and gon on your way," she said and walked away.

Let me find out mama got a man. I know my daddy was rolling over in his grave.

"Alright, Stella, I'm out," I joked.

"Boy, shut up and get out," she laughed.

Today was a beautiful day. Christian didn't want to spend his day down in the dumps, thinking about the 'what if's or what not's'.

He called his wife to see what side of town she was on, so he could know where not to take Asia. "Wasup babe?" he asked.

"How can I help you Christian?" she cut to the chase.

He chuckled. "What y'all up to?" he asked as he switched lanes.

"Just left the spa, headed to the nail shop with Dolly and her daughters," she responded dryly.

"What nail shop y'all going to?" Christian asked.

"Why? Just take her to New York, we're in the city today, so beware," she said and disconnected the call.

Farren turned the radio up, ignoring the look Dolly gave her. The children were too busy entertaining themselves to notice Farren's sudden attitude change. But truth be told, she had been sad all day. She took a deep breath and held back tears that she felt about to pour out of her eyes. "Y'all go on in the nail shop and pick out any color you want," Dolly told all the girls.

"Are you okay?" she asked. Farren broke down. "He doesn't even care that I know; he's just like fuck you and this marriage. He promised to never make me feel like this," she cried.

There was nothing that Dolly could say to make her feel better... there was nothing to say or do. Farren was heartbroken.

"It wasn't supposed to be like this. I did nothing to deserve this, fuckin' nothing. I am a damn good wife." She punched the steering wheel, causing Dolly to jump.

She took a deep breath, and attempted to pep herself up to pull it all together and get her game face on. She needed something, a blunt, a drink, a real hug, some advice. Farren didn't have many friends. Ashley had been too busy with her own life to stop and listen and honestly, Farren didn't want to rain on her parade.

Farren still couldn't believe she tried to kill herself. She was so embarrassed and she felt bad for her own self; she was miserable.

The few friends Farren did have were all connected to Christian somehow, and she wouldn't dare tell those bitches her business. What goes on in the Knight household would stay in the Knight household. Farren then wondered who else knew about HER, besides Greg? Did Christian's sisters know? His business associates? Is that why his receptionist always looked at her crazily? Was she secretly saying, *"bitch your husband is cheating on you"*? Farren's mind was going bananas. She needed to talk to someone and fast.

"Johan!" she shouted.

Dolly was finally convinced that her boss had completely lost her damn mind. "Huh? Who is Johan?" she asked. Farren ignored her question and started the truck back up. "Can you watch the girls? I'm about to go around the corner, I'll be right back. Well text me when y'all are drying," she told Dolly, placing her shades on.

"Are you sure?" Dolly asked, a little worried about Farren.

"Yep, I'm just going right around the corner," she told her. She peeled off as soon as the door met the hinge. She parked her Range parallel in front of the barbershop. "Yo ma, we playing dice right here," some young cat hollered to the fox that exited the 2015 Range Rover. She ignored him.

Farren was flawless. In four months, she would be turning forty years old and she was a force to be reckoned with. Her cheekbones were to die for. She had the facial muscles that models only dreamed of. All she ever needed was a touch of bronze powder. She pulled her hair out of the back of her romper, and straightened her shorts. She was so thick on the bottom.

Farren locked her door, and entered into the barbershop. She scanned the small area for any familiar faces, but didn't recognize anyone. "Is Johan here?" she asked.

"He on the way back ma, he went to get some wings," one of the barbers told her. Farren placed her shades in her purse and took a seat in the waiting area.

She needed to talk to someone she knew she could trust, someone who would keep it real with her. She started to call Dice's brother but thought against it.

"Look what the damn cat done dragged in! When I pulled up I said 'I hope I don't owe nobody no money'. You know I got a nasty gambling habit," he joked.

"Boy shut up, I need to talk to you," she told him.

"Come on, boo." He led her to a basement that one would have never suspected was there.

"Too early for a drink?" he asked.

She shook her head. "It's never too early for a drink, Johan." She fixed herself Cîroc and pineapple juice.

"I haven't seen you in years. How you knew I was here?" he asked.

"I know everything, don't ever forget that," she winked.

He looked her over. "Wasup ma?" he asked. Farren couldn't have wanted money; her nigga was laced, and even if that failed, she had money and her pops did, too.

"The Feds is looking into Chris, but they on my ass though. Even with me dealing with this bullshit, he's cheating on me with a stripper named Asia," she confessed.

"Damn baby," he muttered after a few minutes of silence. "What do you wanna do? You know you can go down for that shit," he told her.

"I'm not worried about those charges, they won't stick. I'm worried about my marriage," she fanned Johan off.

"Farren, you're worried about the wrong thing. Fuck them vows that he not even living by, you need to clear your name," he told her.

"It's being handled, Johan," she said it with finality in her voice. Farren wasn't clueless, she hung with nothing but her older boy cousins growing up, and not to mention, her first boyfriend Dice, taught her well. Either she wasn't speaking on much or it really was being handled.

"So how am I to help with this problem?" he asked out of curiosity.

"Why do y'all cheat?" she asked. Johan was married, happily, she would assume.

"Because women allow us to. Bitches love niggas with wives. It's a thrill," he admitted.

"Does she know, though…that you step out?" she asked above a whisper.

He smirked. "With my wife… I think she rather paints the perfect fairytale in her head. I don't disrespect her, I'm home every night with my kids and I fuck her good. She has no worries."

Farren shrieked. "I don't either, but I feel like with this bitch, he caught feelings," she told him.

"That's his mistake. I'll never put another before my wife. The minute they want more than I'm offering, it's over," he motioned scissors with his hand.

"I can't keep crying about this, I just don't want to lose my husband." She placed her head in her lap. Frustration wasn't a strong enough word to describe her current mental state.

"Don't be anywhere that you're not happy, Farren. I know some real niggas that'll wife you and treat your kids good. You prime pudding round here," he joked.

"Boy, shut up. I gotta go pick up my kids, thank you," she stood up and motioned for a hug.

"Come out tonight. My brother in town visiting," he told her.

"I'm supposed to be flying out to Atlanta in the morning," she shook her head. Farren needed her best friend. She decided to just pop up and cry on her shoulder.

"What's Ashley's fine ass been doing?" he asked.

"Working, working, and working."

"If you change your mind, just text me." He walked her to her car.

"Time is the one thing you can't get back, Farren." He left her with a nugget of wisdom.

The day ended up being a peaceful one. She spent time with her daughters and allowed Dolly and her daughters to get anything they wanted. Being a blessing to others was what made Farren happy.

It was sad that Farren had to stay busy to keep from crying and being depressed, but once night approached, those evil thoughts of suicide kept creeping in the back of her mind. She sat in the floor of her closet, with tears in her eyes. She was tipsy and bored. After blowing Christian's phone up all night and him not answering, she remembered that her friend Johan had invited her out. Farren couldn't remember the last time she'd went to a club, or even went somewhere without her husband and kids. She told herself tonight, she was getting out and enjoying herself. She would deal with her problems tomorrow.

She texted Johan, hoping it wasn't too late to meet up with them to turn up. Farren deserved a good night out.

Farren- What y'all up to?

He replied instantly.

Johan - at my house pre-gaming, fall through!! My wife's stepping out with us tonight.

Farren- Send address, getting dressed.

Farren hopped in the shower. She didn't stay in there long for fear that her pressed hair would curl up. The girls stayed at Dolly's house tonight, so she didn't have to worry about rushing home. Christian probably wasn't coming home anyway. She mentally scanned her walk-in closet looking for something sexy to wear, as she lotioned her body up. The weather was perfect as summer approached, but Farren knew time was of the essence. She didn't have time to try on a million outfits and be indecisive.

She decided on a royal blue pencil dress that fit her body like a glove, and neon Chanel pumps. She decided to only wear a nude lip color and eyeliner. She dabbed Chanel perfume behind her ears and her wrists, and took the Porsche to her friend's home.

Johan home was beautiful. It warmed Farren's heart to see the products of Hardy Projects make something of themselves. Farren didn't know exactly what all Johan was into, but either way it went, they came a long way from the rat-infested projects they grew up in.

Farren parked her car behind a fleet of others. Their house was packed. She knocked on the door and rang the doorbell.

Johan opened the door with a bottle of Rose in his hand. He was already good and drunk. Farren was trying to get on his level tonight. "What up sis," he hugged her when she entered the home. Farren felt someone's eyes peering into her soul, and she looked around but didn't see anyone. "That's my wife up there looking evil...baby, smile. This is my friend Farren I be talking about," he said.

"Jo, you do not be talking about her, stop lying," she said.

"Man, for real. We got a lawyer from Hardy. Man, your mama always bragging on you when I slide through the hood," he said.

Sadness swept over me, and I told myself I needed to go visit my mother one day soon, before it was too late.

His wife stood over the banister throwing me hella shade. She was probably wondering was I really was his "sister". But Farren didn't know his wife, and she didn't know what she was about or how she operated. Mari trusted her husband and had heard about Farren over the years, and not just from her husband.

"Come up here, I'm still getting dressed," his wife shouted over the banister. Farren took off her heels and left them at the bottom of the steps. Johan respected Farren and looked to her as a sister, but he was still a man, and him turning his head when that ass was jiggling as she ran up the steps was out the question.

"Hi girl, give me a hug. We should have been met," she told her. Farren wondered was she being fake, but she didn't say anything. She offered her a church hug and left it at that.

Farren always thought that she and Christian's home was immaculate, but this bedroom was exquisite. "I love this closet," she complimented.

"Girl, thank you. I barely wear half of that shit," she said from the bathroom.

Farren observed her as she moved around. She was a full-blooded Puerto Rican, short and thick, definitely Johan's type.

"Hey, didn't you use to run track? I knew I knew you," Farren said.

"Yes I did. Girl, I'm so damn out of shape now," she laughed.

"So how many kids do you have?" Mari asked after she poured the both of them a glass of wine.

"Three, two girls and a boy," she told her. "How many kids do you and Johan have now? I know y'all had a boy recently," Farren responded.

"Girl, four bad ass kids. My husband said you're a lawyer, how are you handling both?"

"As in raising my kids and working? Like everybody else does. I do way more than that," Farren laughed.

Mari looked over her again but remained quiet. She was a housewife and did nothing more than that. She desired independence, but never spoke up for herself. With her being a stay-at-home wife, she didn't know much about social clubs and organizations she could join where her and her children could benefit. Farren put her up on game. "I'm so glad you ran into Johan. Girl, I have no friends," she laughed.

Farren joined her, "honey me neither," they clapped hands. They got to know each other better and before the clock struck midnight, they realized they had too much in common. It seemed as if they both were happy to have met each other.

"Girl, this ringgggggggggggg." Mari grabbed Farren's hand and openly admired her wedding ring.

"Girl, please," she fanned her off.

She smiled. She knew that comment all too well. "It comes with the territory." She offered her a smile, "like been there done that".

She was dressed sexily in a pencil skirt and corset like top. She was in her late thirties but after four children, Mari damn sure still had it.

"You ready? Jo texted me three times asking where we at," she asked after they took a few shots.

"Yeah, you can drive my car I don't know where it is," she told Mari.

"The driver is going to take us." She smiled and led Farren out the side door into a dark Escalade. She clearly had to be out the loop; she didn't know Johan was doing it like that.

The party was turned the fuck up. They were having the time of their life. Farren had taken way too many shots and her and Mari were popping bottle after bottle. Her sisters joined them shortly, and they were all turned up in their private section.

"Jo's brother is here. Waitress, bring another round," she said, and placed a hundred dollar bill in the lady's pouch. This was the waitress' lucky night. She didn't expect to come in and make enough to cover bills and go shopping, in a matter of one hour.

"Sis, my brother let you out looking this good?" Johan's brother grabbed Mari's waist and kissed her cheek before hugging her sisters.

"I've never seen you before," he told Farren, all in her space.

"Yes you have," she told him.

"Where you from? I don't know you." He looked in her eyes. He had Farren feeling something...she just didn't know what.

"Hardy projects. I stayed under y'all," she informed him.

"Farren... girl you ain't knock-kneed no more. Did you ever go to college? You was the fastest girl in the neighborhood," he joked.

She nodded her head. "Farren Knight, attorney at law," she smirked, and held out her hand for a handshake. Jonte didn't even look the same. He was arrested for drugs when they were younger, and she hadn't seen him since. She wasn't even sure of his age. She and Johan was a year apart, so he had to be about thirty-six because he was younger than his brother.

"Lawyer? You came a long way from Hardy. What's your friend name? Umm, lil' thick mama," he snapped his fingers trying to remember her name.

"Ashley. She's well, she lives in Atlanta," Farren caught him up.

"That's wasup. I'ma go holler at a few of my niggas. Don't leave without telling me goodbye," he said, getting into her space once again.

Mari looked at her and winked. She laughed and took another shot. Before she knew it, Johan was walking them to the car. "I really needed tonight. I never go anywhere, but work and home," she slurred. Johan laughed as he rolled a blunt. "Anytime sis. We be at the house doing shit, but my brother back in the city, so we had to go out tonight," he lit the blunt.

"Wake your ass up, Mari." He slapped his wife's thigh, and helped her out the car.

"We're doing lunch Tuesday, don't forget," Farren told her new friend, as she unlocked her door.

"Johan, don't let her drive, she is too threw," Mari hissed.

"Ma, you can't drive. We have plenty of room, sleep some of that drank off." She checked her phone. Christian hadn't bothered to call or text, and she knew her children were safe, so she took them up on their offer and crashed in the guest room, fully dressed.

On the other side of town, Christian was peeling out of bed with Asia. He woke up to pee and saw that he a hundreds of missed calls from Farren. The first thought that went through his mind was something either happened with the kids or those agents were fucking with her again. "I hate to see you go," she told him. Slipping on one of his t-shirts, he stumbled over all the shopping bags on the floor in her condo.

"Me too, boo. I'll be over here this week," he told her honestly, as he kissed her face.

"Get back in the bed, get some sleep," he instructed her. She sadly obeyed him.

Christian did one twenty getting home, only to enter the five car garage with one car missing: his Porsche. Where in the fuck was Farren? He called her phone all night. All he thought about was the police getting to her. He searched her name and googled crime reports but nothing came up. He called her phone all night, praying for the best.

It was then that he realized he couldn't leave his wife or his children. He had to be there to protect them like he promised to do when they said their vows and every time she was in labor.

Before he knew it, the sun was shining and he blamed himself for being laid up with someone else, while his wife could possibly be in danger. His lawyer wasn't answering and he didn't want to show his face at the police station. The alarm sounded, the fridge opened and closed, and he sat up on the couch. From where he sat, he could see Farren taking her heels off. He couldn't believe the dress she had on and the time she was coming in the house.

"Where you been?" he asked.

She jumped. "You scared me." She held her heart.

"I asked you a question."

"I went to some club with my friends," she told him and went up the steps.

Christian followed her closely. "What friends?" he asked. Farren didn't have any friends; she was at home by 8 and sleep by ten every night.

"From hardy, you don't know them." She sounded annoyed and hung over.

"You hangin' with people from hardy? Since when? What you got going on?" he asked.

"Not everyone from Hardy is strung out, okay. Some of us made it out of there. I'm sorry we all didn't have it good coming up," she threw shots. Farren wasn't stuntin Christian's ass. She wanted to wash last night off of her and go to sleep.

She entered the shower, acting as if he wasn't even there. "So if you did go out, why are you just now getting home? Since when do you stay out, and where are the kids?" he questioned.

"And why was you blowing my phone up, Farren. I thought something happened to you," he continued. She ignored him and smothered her ass and titties in body wash, and for a millisecond, Christian wondered if she had been with a man.

"With Dolly. They didn't want to come home and I was too drunk to drive, so I took a nap and slept some of it off. Anymore questions, Christian?" she told him with her back turned to him. Since when did Farren talk to him this way? Just the other day she was trying to kill herself because of him.

"You slept where?" he leaned on the sink waiting for an answer.

"Why the fuck does it matter? You think I'm a dummy? You didn't call me until 4:30 which means you got home and saw I wasn't here. Stop trying to play me," she yelled. Christian pulled back the shower door and it damn near cracked. He grabbed her neck roughly. "You better watch your tone. Don't forget who I am, Farren." He had to remind her exactly who the fuck he was.

Farren tore away from his embrace. "Fuck you," she yelled and threw her washcloth at him. He grabbed her neck again and kissed her in her mouth. Ignoring the taste of liquor and using his other hand, he separated her legs and stuck his fingers in her pussy. Farren's vagina creamed instantly. It had been months since their last encounter. "Give this pussy away if you want to," he told her.

She rolled her eyes and fought to let out a moan.

"Stop fighting it. Daddy miss his pussy." Christian completely forgot that his mouth had just been between the legs of someone else, and he hadn't brushed his teeth or showered yet. His mind had been strictly on finding Farren. Yet still, he got down on his knees in their walk in shower, fully clothed, and ate the shit out of his wife's pussy. She came and erupted over and over again. He had to show her that before she could even think about leaving him, it wasn't happening.

He bit on her clit, causing Farren to exhale and moan out in pleasure. He glanced at his wife only to see her eyes were closed shut. He didn't know if those were tears or drops from the shower head. He cut the shower off, stepped out and undressed then led his wife to their bedroom. Christian opened her legs preparing to enter her. But Farren couldn't dare to look into his eyes. Farren flipped over and got on all fours. Christian didn't argue with her. In his mind, pussy was pussy. He entered her slowly and stroked her middle. "Fuck me," she shouted. He was surprised to hear demands from her. She usually wanted slow lovemaking, candles and music. Farren brought her ass up higher, spreading her ass cheeks and begged to be fucked. She said it over and over again. Christian granted her wishes, their lovemaking.....well fucking, didn't last long. She came and shortly after, he pulled out of his wife and spilled his release all over their carpet. After gaining composure, he went to the bathroom to get himself together and brought a hot towel back to their bedroom to wash his wife up.

"Open up," he said huskily.

"I got it," she told him and went back to the shower, then brushed her teeth.

"Since when you washed our lovemaking off?" he asked once she returned to the room in a towel.

"Since you came home in a car that we didn't purchase, so I'm assuming that's the car you bought her," she told him without even looking his way.

Christian was dumbfounded. He was so worried about getting home to his wife and children, that he didn't even notice he was driving Asia's candy red Mercedes Benz.

"Baby," he went to her.

"Save it," she told him and left the room.

Farren woke up to voices, laughter and chatter. She tossed and turned in her sleep and realized she wasn't able to return back to sleep.

She slid on the Nike leggings that were on the floor, and went to see what was going on in her home.

"Farren, Christian said you weren't feeling well, so we went on and started cooking," Chloe said as she took a pan of what smelled like mac and cheese out of the oven.

"I didn't know we were having dinner here today. I would have had everything together," she told her sisters-in-law and mother in law.

"It's okay, the table is set. Just pull that wine out of the fridge," her sister-in-law, Courtney, told her.

Farren went to tell the children and her nephews to come fix their plates. "We don't eat without saying grace, y'all know better," Christian's mother scolded. The children were in the kitchen eating, while the adults sat in the dining room.

"God, we thank you for this day bringing the family together to fellowship, thank you for the meal and the hands that prepared it. God, today let us remember why you brought families together on Sunday. Bring peace and happiness into this home, in your son's Jesus name I pray, and my children join me in saying, Amen," she concluded. Everyone looked at her but didn't dare say a word.

"Pass the greens," Chloe said to her husband.

"Courtney, I heard your garden is looking better than mine," their mother joked.

She nodded. "I just picked some tomatoes and squash yesterday," she told the table.

"Christian, how is the center going?" Chloe asked.

"It's going good," he told his sister.

Farren drunk more wine than she ate food. She wasn't in the mood to be fake around her in-laws. She loved them dearly but the tension between her and Christian couldn't be ignored.

"This was good, ma," Christian told his mother. She smiled.

"Farren, your birthday is coming. I know you're doing something for the big 4-0?" his mother asked Farren.

She swallowed her food and shook her head. "I don't have any plans, just probably visiting Ashley," she told them.

"We will probably go out of town when she gets back," he told the family.

Farren could have been petty, but she was grown and it wasn't in her to embarrass herself or her husband. She constantly checked the clock to see when was this Sunday dinner coming to an end, after realizing they weren't in a rush to leave.

She excused herself from the table to get her children ready for bed. The kids had school in the morning, and Farren was determined to get her case back. She worked too damn hard on it.

"She is so threw with you, it's all in her face," Chloe whispered to the table. Her husband told her to mind her business.

"Shut up, she just got a lot going on with work," Christian assured his family. He hoped that Farren didn't want a divorce. Christian was now having a change of heart, after their sex session this morning.

"Christian, you should be embarrassed," Chloe continued.

"Embarrassed for what? Chloe what do you know? Nothing at all." He stood up and started clearing the table. His sister pushed his buttons sometimes. He wasn't easily angered, but she was so damn annoying.

After his family had left, he went behind Farren and made sure the kids were tucked in the bed. He dreaded entering their room.

"Farren," he called out her name. She paused the television and cocked her head in his direction.

"You good?" he asked.

"After you get to the bottom of this bullshit with those federal agents, I would like a divorce," she said.

He wondered what had gotten into her. She went to some stupid club with those hoodlums from Hardy Projects, now all of a sudden she wanted a divorce.

"No," Christian told her.

"Are you going to stop cheating?" she asked.

"You need to focus on your career." He attempted to change the subject.

"Where did we go wrong? You have yet to answer the million dollar question. Christian let's be honest with each other here....please, can we be honest with each other. I'm a big girl, I can handle it. Just tell me, do you love her? Is that who you want to be with? Because if so, it's okay, just don't string me along anymore. I deserve to be with someone who actually wants to be with me," Farren stated with confidence. In fact, it was the first thing she said with confidence all year. Her voice was no longer shaking and she didn't utter or mumble; she spoke with finality. Who wanted to be with someone who barely touched them or made eye contact with them? Who wanted to love a man who didn't love or respect his "woman"? Who wanted to chase and beg someone for simple gestures of affection?

The hardest part of letting go is letting go. Farren believed that she had done all she could do to save their marriage and if it had now come to an end, then she would appreciate the lesson learned and somehow place the pieces of her life back together. But when a man doesn't even hide his side bitch anymore, it's out in the open for friends and family to know but not speak on the situation, then yeah, it's time to leave. Farren was beautiful and she knew it, but after years of researching ways to keep your husband happy, tips on spicing the bedroom up, and other bullshit that could be found on Google, she was over it. Separating their children or what others thought didn't bother him, and their vows apparently meant nothing to him. Farren had to get her life together. She'd spent countless nights crying and drinking. Her career that she put so much time into was failing, and she was losing case after case. Her dreams were turning into nightmares and she couldn't recall the last time she'd actually put on clothes and enjoyed herself. She wanted her mind and heart back.

She gave him one more chance to answer the question before she decided that she was filing divorce.

"Farren, I don't believe in divorce and I told you that, so get that out your head. There is no leaving this marriage or this house or your family," he told her. This nigga was crazy.

"But you're able to buy bitches cars and come in when you want? But I'm forced to stay loyal to a man who isn't loyal to me?" she spat.

"Don't ever forget our vows," he told her.

"Christian, you're so hypocritical. Don't you forget our vows. Just admit that you are sleeping around," she yelled.

"Get some rest, I'll be back later." He cut the light off and left their room.

She hopped out of their bed and walked up on him, hair all over her head, and in a big t-shirt. She mushed her husband in the back of the head. "You think you gon just keep walking up outta here whenever the fuck you get ready? Let me tell you something. I've been here; don't you forget that while you're chasing these young hoes. I stayed up with you at night, I supported your dreams. Don't you ever fuckin' forget it," she spat.

He just looked at her. Farren wasn't done though. "You don't get to hurt me, I've done nothing to deserve this," she cried.

He stared, speechless. No words came out of his mouth and his facial expression never changed. He just looked. "Where did we go wrong? What did I do? Christian, what happened to us?" she asked him. Farren had a lot of questions; however, he never had an answer. Christian knew she wasn't the one to blame. Farren did nothing wrong. She loved him unconditionally and remained faithful over the years. In the urban dictionary, under the definition of "ride or die", Farren's picture was probably there. Ride or Die of the Century award went to her. She constantly put him before her, it was obvious. Her career was suffering due to the bullshit he was putting her through. As much as Christian loved his wife, his heart desired to be elsewhere at that present moment. Christian left his wife crying on the steps in their home.

Farren

Despite last night's events, Farren woke up in a good ass mood. She told herself that she was going to get the Darrian Morris case back; it was her case. She was the one that took the case before it gained so much exposure. Her firm looked at him like a rich hoodlum and threw the case on her just because their skin color matched. Farren searched high and low for a parking space at the courthouse. Her plan was to observe Morgan in court before approaching Darrian asking to be put back on the case, because ultimately it was his decision. Her cell phone rung and it was Robin. Farren thought to herself, *what the fuck did she want.* Farren had been ignoring all her phone calls. Even though she had put her suicide attempt behind her, she didn't feel comfortable talking or befriending Robin. She had seen her in her weakest and it made her uncomfortable to talk to her or be around her.

Farren answered the phone anyway. "Hello?" She couldn't find a parking spot for nothing and she was getting mad.

"Hi Farren, how are you?" Robin asked cheerfully.

"I'm well, headed into court. What's up?" Farren wasn't in the mood to have conversation.

"Just wondering when are you free? Maybe we can do drinks. We have yet to finish your first session." She sounded pressed and Farren wasn't feeling that.

"Umm, I'm not sure. Really busy right now with this case," I told her.

"Oh okay, well I'll call you this weekend or I can stop by the house," she suggested.

"Hmm, okay, yeah, I will be in touch. Have a good day." Farren hung the phone up and pulled into a handicap parking spot. She could afford the parking ticket but she couldn't afford to lose this case.

Three hours later and Farren was getting back into her truck with the biggest smile plastered across her face that she had in a long time. Darrian damn near begged her to take back on the case. He said Morgan's voice was annoying and he had already fucked her twice. The girl was officially bad for business.

Farren called her assistant. "Dolly, whatever your plans are for tonight, cancel them. We have one week until the next court date and we have to get the judge on our side," she said.

"Umm okay, when did you get another case?" Dolly asked.

"I got the Darrian Morris case back, so meet me at my house. I'm about to swing through the office and get my files and I'll meet you at the house. Bring the girls and pick up some pizza," she casted off orders.

Farren felt like she had her mojo back and it felt so good. After loading all of files in the back of her trunk, she went to close it.

"Mrs. Knight, what's been up?" the federal agent asked, holding on to the trunk.

She was determined not to let anything ruin her good mood. "Working, how can I help you gentlemen today?" she smiled.

"One name, we just need one name," he told her.

"I don't know anything, and if y'all are really doing your research, you would know that," she told them truthfully. Farren refused to let whatever Christian had going on mess with her career. She had the power to possibly go from just being well known in Philadelphia and New York, to being placed in the category with Johnnie Cochran, Benjamin Crump and her idol, Barbara Jordan. She prayed for days like this and she didn't plan on sleeping until she had the perfect presentation to win.

Mari called her phone while she was on the highway to pick her children up.

"What you doing girl?" she asked.

"Nothing, just got my case back the one I was telling you about", she told her.

"I know you're happy, I am happy too. I was calling to see if you wanted to get some drinks. I need to get out this house. I'm bored," she said.

"Get a bottle, and meet me at my house; bring the kids. Honey I'm about to put you to work," she joked with Mari, but she was very serious. Farren didn't understand how that girl did nothing all day but cook and clean. She wished Christian would fix his lips to tell her she didn't have to work. He already knew what the answer was.

"I got my degree in business administration," she told her.

"Mari, are you serious? Yeah, bring your ass. Call me when you're outside so I can buzz you in," I told my new friend and hung the phone up.

Farren caught herself yawning, but she quickly sat up straight in her truck. She had a lot of work to do and sleep was for the weak. She picked her children up. "How was school?" she asked.

"Boring as usual. Can we go to the mall this weekend?" Carren asked.

"Did you pass your math test?" Farren asked. Yes, her children were spoiled. They didn't have a need or a want, but they raised their children on very strict principles, respect and education.

Always respect yourself first, respect your parents and elders, and respect those around you whether they have more or less then you. Farren refused to raise ignorant children. Her children would be well-rounded. She tried her hardest to keep them off a high horse.

"I don't know yet," she told her mom.

"Okay, well I'll email your teacher when I get home." Farren wasn't born yesterday nor was she stupid. That girl took that test last week and never brought up a grade. If Carren made an 'A' on a test, she would nag the shit out of Christian for a new trinket or pair of Uggs. When she made a bad grade, she would stay clear from her parents.

"I got a 'C', dang," she said.

"Dang? Lil' girl, who are you talking to? I would hate to have to remind you who I am today" Farren fussed.

Noel giggled in the backseat. "And what you back there laughing about lil' mama? What you learn today?" she asked her youngest daughter.

"About the presidents," she said.

"Mmm hmm, okay buckle up. I have a lot of work to do tonight. Dolly is bringing pizza and Mari, my friend, y'all don't know her, she has daughters around y'all age and she's coming too. So y'all can have a lil' play date," she told her children.

"Mike, how was school son?" she asked her son. Farren made a mental note to remind Christian to spend more time with his son.

"It was cool, ma," he said.

***

The clock struck two, signifying that she had been up for hours working on the case, but sleep wasn't in her plans tonight. "Farren, this case...I think you can use this to show relevance," Mari said.

She was pouring herself another cup of coffee. "Let me see." She went back to the dining room. They had transformed her dining room into a mini office. Pots of coffee had been brewing all night. Farren switched out of her suit for a t-shirt and leggings, her hair pulled up into a messy bun.

"Mari! Oh my God. Yes! Ugh, I love you," she hugged her and screamed. Farren sat at the table and scanned the document with a highlighter, making notes to include in her opening argument.

"Girl, I am about to go. My husband is blowing my phone up," Mari stood.

"Aww okay, I know how that can be," she told her friend. Mari offered her a weak smile. There were no signs of Christian nor had he called or texted, to check on her or the kids.

"Get home safe and text me when you get there," I told her.

"I really had fun tonight. Let me know if I can help again. When do you present?" she asked, after she went to wake up her children so they could head home.

"Girl, next week. I am so nervous, but I got this," I signified the praise hands.

"Yes you do. Call me tomorrow, you owe me lunch," she told her and gave Farren a hug.

Farren had told Dolly to crash in one of the spare bedrooms, hours ago. She was falling asleep at the table and was in Farren's way.

After seeing her guests out, she went right back to work practicing her oratorical. Her phone started vibrating and it took Farren a few minutes to locate it. Her dining room was a mess.

She saw that she had one missed call from Mari and zero missed calls from her husband.

"Hey girl, you called me?" she asked.

"Yeah, when I pulled out of your driveway, it was a car like parked right by your mailbox. That shit ain't look right so I was just letting you know. I waited until the gate closed all the way before I pulled off," she told her, sounding extremely concerned.

"Thanks girl, let me call my husband and see where he is. He probably still at the office," Farren attempted to make everything sound good.

"Okay," she said and they ended the call.

Farren fished through her purse and retrieved her gun and sat it on the table. She then went to lock the front door and turned the alarm on. She went to the living room and with the push of a few buttons on the remote control, she was able to access every single camera that was on their premises. Farren saw the black Buick parked "discreetly" at the end of their driveway. She didn't know who the hell it was and she wasn't going to wait to find out.

After checking on her children and seeing they were fast asleep, she called her husband's phone.

"Hello?" he said sounding sleepy.

"Umm, hello, where are you? It is 2:45 in the morning?" she asked.

"Wasup?" he ignored her.

"Wasup?" she asked.

"Farren, is everything okay?" He sounded irritated and mad that she'd interrupted his sleep.

"No it is not. Why you're laid up with that bitch, it's some black car parked by the gate," she told him, matter-of-factly. Christian could only imagine, how scrunched up her face was right now, neck rolling and everything. Farren was such a firecracker.

"That's somebody that works for me, you good. Get some sleep," he yawned.

"Christian, since when is it okay for you to not come home? When did we separate?" she asked.

"Goodnight" he said and hung the phone up.

It didn't register in her brain until three minutes later that one, her husband was elsewhere, and two, with everything that was going on, he hired a security guard instead of keeping us safe himself. And then three, he hung up in her face. Something had to give and it had to give real soon. Farren's day was too productive for her to allow Christian's blatant disrespect to piss her off. She had a great day and was one step closer to making history. She turned the lights off downstairs and went to bathe and prepare for yet another long day in preparation in the Darrian Morris case. Farren woke up in a sweat and she found herself on her knees praying in the middle of the night. "God please send me a sign or a wonder. I cannot live like this anymore. God, I know you have more in store for me then this heartbreak. Fix it Jesus," she whispered, with tears in her eyes. She wiped her face and lay back down and prayed that she could learn to sleep in peace without her husband lying next to her.

And God was on her side. Farren slept so good the kids were late to school. "I'm sorry y'all, have a good day. Your auntie is going to pick y'all up today," she told them after she signed them in at the attendance office.

"Mari, wake up! You riding with me today," she screamed into the phone.

"Bitch, what time is it?" she muttered into the phone.

"It's 9:30, you didn't take your kids to school?"

"No, the house keeper did," she said. Farren wanted to ask her why she had a housekeeper if she didn't have a job, but that wasn't her business.

"Oh okay, well I'm on the way," she told her and hung up before she could protest.

Farren hopped out of her truck and ran into the corner store to get a bottle of water. "So you not gon speak Miss lady?" a familiar voice said to her.

Farren turned around. "Honey I ain't even see you, wasup," she said smiling.

"I must look good this morning, what you smiling at me for? You miss me?" the voice asked.

"Jonte please, you ain't all that," she laughed. Farren knew she was lying through her teeth. Jonte was fine as hell. He towered over her, and his smile was big and inviting. The curls atop his head... for a second Farren pictured running her manicured fingers through his hair while they laid in the bed, watching whatever he wanted to watch.

"Now you know you lying," he told her. "I'm paying for my stuff and hers. You need some gas?" he asked.

Farren was insulted. "Baby I'm on full, do you need some gas?" she shot back.

"Okay Miss independent, I hear you," he smiled at her. Damn, was that her pussy getting wet? Farren had to get out the corner store. He had her feeling something she had no business experiencing.

"What you doing today?" he asked.

"I have errands to run. I'm pulling your sister-in-law out the house today," Farren told him.

"Good, good. She don't go nowhere," he said.

"You looking good. I'm loving this dress on you, boo," he slapped her thigh. Farren looked in her side mirror. Damn she still had it. She was a few months shy from turning forty, but baby girl was still turning heads and breaking necks.

"I threw this on," she fanned him off.

"It don't matter, you're still beautiful," he told her.

"Let me get out of here," Farren told him.

"when you gon let me at least text you good morning and goodnight?" he asked.

"I'm married, I don't think my husband would like that," she told him. Just because Christian was doing his dirt and spitting all over their vows, two wrongs never made a right.

"Respect. Well you be safe and enjoy your day," he told her and walked towards pump five where she saw an Audi parked with tinted windows.

Farren bit her tongue and asked God to remove those wicked thoughts from her head. Jonte was sexy, yes indeed, but he had nothing on the infamous Christian Knight.

With her husband on her mind, she called his phonc.

"Hello?" he appeared to be more alert then he was last night.

"Hello husband," Farren greeted him.

"Hi wife, how are you?" he asked

"I'm well, working. Are you free for lunch today? You know there was a time when we went to lunch at least three times a week" she asked.

"Actually I am not. I have meetings all day, ALL day. I'm swamped." Before responding, she evaluated his tone and concluded that this was the probably the first truth her husband said in months.

"Okie dokie then boo, I was just asking. Christian I miss you," she admitted.

"I know Farren, look I'm busy, I'll try and stop by tomorrow," he rushed her off the phone.

"Try? Don't worry about it."

When was it okay if you didn't stay at home? What marriage did y'all know operated under two different households? Farren didn't know what the hell Christian had going on and she wasn't feeling it. But due to the fact that time was not on her side with the Darrian Morris case, she had to place her emotions on the back burner and her money on the front.

Farren knocked and knocked once she arrived at Mari's residence and no one came to the door, not even the housekeeper. Farren rang the doorbell and called Mari's phone back to back. She didn't see how someone could sleep past twelve. Farren didn't even know what noon looked like. Her days were always long and productive. She worked out, went to work, cooked dinner, planted seeds in her garden and most importantly, she was very active in her community.

"Who is it?" a ruffled voice asked from behind the door.

"It's Farren Knight," she said cheerfully. Locks were heard unclicking. "What you doing here?" Johan asked. He came to the door with a gun in his hand.

"Why are y'all still sleep? I called Mari an hour ago and told her to get dressed," she said once she stepped into the home.

"That girl knocked out. You worked her like a slave last night," he joked.

"No I did not. We got a long day today," Farren told Johan.

"I'ma go wake her up, give her thirty minutes," he said, and jogged back up the steps.

As Farren patiently waited, she made her dentist and eye doctor appointments along with her children's. She made a hair appointment and scheduled other important appointments. She was getting herself together and back on track.

"Girl I'm sorry, you ready?" Mari came down the steps dressed comfortably in jeans and a blazer.

"I love this blazer. Good morning," she told her new friend.

"Girl, this damn thang so old honey."

"Babe, I'm gone," she yelled up the steps.

"Here you go, we have a very long day ahead of us," Farren handed her a coffee and a bag full of donuts.

"Hmm... thank you. What we gotta do?" she asked.

"Well first, we are going to meet with my client, then swing by the office to drop off these files, go to the Boys & Girls club, stop by one of my colleague's book signing - girl she wrote a real good book. And then we are going to a charity event at the art gallery," she ran down today's agenda.

"Oh shit, I shouldn't have worn these red bottoms," Mari complained.

"You're good. It's going to be a productive day," Farren smiled. If they were going to be friends, Mari had to be beneficial and doing something with her life. Although motherhood was a full-time job, Farren didn't believe in hanging with anyone who had absolutely nothing going on. By the end of the week, she wanted to help her new friend find her purpose.

The duo started their day late, but they went all in as soon as Farren pulled out of Mari's driveway. Hours later, everything was crossed out on the to-do list, and the two were at dinner reminiscing on a very successful day.

"Farren, now I ain't no groupie bitch, but I've never seen stuff like that today. Art galleries... book signings. I mean, me and Johan go to nice shit but them women... I just feel so motivated right now" she said.

Farren raised her wine glass to her friend. "That's what it's all about. Now they're a lil' bourgeois, I'm not even going to lie to you, but we all support each other and everybody got something going on. I keep telling you, you better flip your husband money," Farren encouraged her.

"I could if I wanted to, but I like being home. I love what I do," she said. Farren realized that everyone wasn't workaholics and some women were okay with being housewives, and Mari was one of them. She didn't judge her or knock her for it at all either.

"I understand that," Farren told her.

"Girl, no you do not, but it's okay," she laughed and shook her head.

"My husband been blowing me up. Honey, we gone have to do this once a week, not every day," she said seriously. Johan called her all day just to say I love you and I miss you. A twinge of jealousy ran through Farren for just a second. No one called her, no one checked on her anymore.

"That's so sweet. I remember those days," Farren said truthfully.

"What's up with you and your husband?" Mari asked. She had been itching to get the truth. Farren looked sad and miserable to her.

"We're just going through a really rough patch right now, but we will be okay," Farren said with little hope and assurance.

"Girl, and if y'all don't, leave his ass. You pretty as hell and you got your own money, honey, boom," she told her.

"You would leave your husband, if...never mind." Farren never has been one to pillow talk, or to let outsiders in on her problems.

"If what? If he cheated on me or stopped loving me?" she asked. Farren looked up at her and wondered how she knew.

"The streets talk. I know your husband supposed to be some untouchable man. But his girl is from my cousin's hood," Mari said.

Farren sipped her wine. "You know her?" she asked, scared to get the answer.

"Nah, but I know she's fucking your husband," she said matter-of-factly.

"I'm so embarrassed. Let me get the check." She threw the napkin in her food that she barely touched. But Farren no longer had an attitude.

"Why? We're women. Wasup? No need to be embarrassed, trust me. I've been through worst shit with my husband, honey, trust me," she told her.

"And you're still with him?" Farren asked.

"Oh, I can't name these bitches by name. They should know you but you should never know them. That's where your husband messed up," she said.

Cheating shouldn't be acceptable by any means. "I don't agree. Why do they gotta cheat? We don't even do anything wrong. Mari, I am a good wife, I promise I am. I gave this man my life," she said.

Mari reached over the table and grabbed Farren's hand. "And that's where *you* messed up, boo. Why is he your life? You are your own person," she told her.

Farren had tears in her eyes and she didn't bother wiping them away. "I can't be without him, I just can't," she shook her head.

"Farren, does he want to be with you?" she asked.

Farren took a deep breath, exhaled and shook her head. The tears were really coming down now.

Mari reached into her purse and tossed two hundred dollar bills on the table and helped her friend up from the table. Farren hated appearing weak, she really did. She remembered the first time Christian ever lied to her. She would never ever forget it.

"Girl, let me call you back. I gotta prepare for my night. I'm about to make love to my husband like never before," she told her best friend.

"What do you have planned? I need some tips," Ashley inquired.

"Let me find out you have a man," Farren joked.

"Anyways, mind your business. What's on the agenda tonight?" she asked.

"Well, after I put the children to bed, I am grilling lobster tails and broiling the biggest steaks you have ever seen, honey! I have some wine chilling as we speak, and an aged bottle of Hennessy. When he walks in the door, I'll be greeting him in this silk negligee, girl, with these white pumps I can barely walk in. After dinner, I will be feeding him strawberries and whip cream, followed by a personal show from yours truly. Then I'll be sucking his dick until my jaws lock up." Farren burst out laughing. It was funny to her because she used to hate sucking dick, but she couldn't keep Christian's balls from down her throat.

"Turn up then sister, enjoy your night. I love you." Ashley told her. She didn't sound as excited for Farren, but she couldn't sit there and dwell on it. She had a lot to do before Christian got home.

Farren went to run Carren and Michael's bath water. Normally she wouldn't bathe them together, but tonight the brother and sister would be sharing the same bubbles and rubber ducks.

Farren snapped pictures of the children in the tub and sent them to her husband.

"Come on mama's babies." She helped them out of the tub and dried them off quickly. Carren fell asleep quickly as long as her television was on. Farren read her a bedtime story and listened to Carren stumble on saying her prayers, but at least she was trying.

It was Michael who took forever to fall asleep. "Baby, lay down, no more jumping." He never calmed down. Michael would tear her house up all day and all night. He wrote on the walls, pulled on the curtains, peed on himself. Michael was a very bad child, and none of the family understood who he got that from because Christian was a good child growing up, and so was Farren.

"Michael get in this bed, now I'm not going to tell you anymore," she fussed. She didn't have long to straighten up the house, make the bed, take a bath, do her makeup and prepare dinner.

Farren regretted spending so long in the office. In truth she should have been home.

Forty-five minutes later, her son eyes finally became heavy, and before she knew it, he was snuggled up under the covers with his favorite toy truck that he insisted on sleeping with every night. Farren dashed out of the room, throwing the kids toys in the closet. She didn't have time to take her time straightening up. Instead of standing outside flipping steaks and lobsters, she made a quick deal of spaghetti and salad. Although her husband preferred steak tonight, he would have to do with the spaghetti. Farren took her time bathing and shaving. She wanted him to inhale her fragrance before he licked her. She bathed in her favorite Gucci body wash. After washing her body, she applied light makeup, lotioned up and slid into her lingerie. Farren then pulled out the shopping bags from earlier, and placed candles and rose petals all over the house, creating a romantic scene for her husband. Between the two, she didn't know the last time they did something special for each other. Christian had been working tirelessly, and Farren was climbing her way to the top of the corporate ladder.

An hour or two, maybe three later, Farren blew Christian's phone up, wondering where he was. She began to panic thinking something was wrong. Farren didn't meddle in his private affairs regarding his life as "The Connect", but when he didn't answer the phone and ignored her text messages, she assumed he was probably in jail, or worse, DEAD.

Before Farren could come up with a concrete decision on what to do next, her cell phone rung in her hands and she saw that Greg was calling her. She instantly thought the worst. "He...hello?" she spoke into the phone.

"Farren, hey how you doing? I hate to call you this late, but can you put Chris on the phone? It's an emergency," he said.

"Christian is not here, Greg," she told him sternly.

The phone was silent for a few seconds. "Oh, I'm tripping. He did say he was gon be at the office late," he tried to clean it up.

"Goodnight Greg." Farren hung the phone up, embarrassed as hell.

She didn't want to think her husband was out doing something or better yet laid up with another bitch, but her woman's intuition told her she was right.

Farren wiped tears back as she threw the hot pot of spaghetti in the trash. She didn't even care if the heat burned the plastic trash bag. She was pissed off.

Farren sat at the dining room table, and sipped wine til the wee hours of the morning.

Four fifty two. Her husband walked into the house that they lived in with their two children at FOUR FIFTY TWO.

"Where have you been Chrissy?" Farren asked.

"Shit you scared me," he held his heart, and turned the lights on.

"Why are you sitting in the dark? Babe, why are you still up?" he asked.

She stared at him. "Farren, are you drunk?" he asked, removing the wine bottle from the table.

She remained silent. "What are you mad about now?" he asked.

"Christian, four fifty two. FOUR FIFTY TWO, really?" she asked.

"It's been a long day boo, so please don't start," he said.

"Where the fuck were you, and please don't lie to me," she asked.

"Why are you questioning me? You need to lower your voice when you talking to me," he told her.

"No, you need to walk your black ass in here at FOUR FIFTY TWO like ain't nothing wrong with that." She hopped out of the dining room chair, causing it to fall on the floor.

"Farren, for real? You need to gon and go to bed," he warned her.

"Or what nigga? What your lying, cheating ass going to do?" She threw a bottle at him. Farren knew how to push Christian's buttons.

"Really? I'm going to bed. I don't have time for this," he turned away. She got up behind him in six inch heels and all.

He turned around. "What do you have on?" he asked.

"If your ass would have come home before four fifty two, I wouldn't have this on right now. Look around Christian." She cut the lights on so he could see the set up.

His face bore it all. For one, he felt like shit, and two, he wore a face of guilt and shame.

"Damn boo, I'm sorry. Why didn't you tell me?" he asked, wrapping his arms around her waist.

"It's called a surprise," she smacked her lips

"Aye ma, lose the attitude. I don't like all that," he told her and meaning every single word. Farren didn't want to argue with her husband all night. He looked and smelled too good.

"I'm so mad at you right now", she pouted.

"Let daddy make it better," he told her, and guided her into their bedroom, where Christian erased any thoughts of him cheating on her far, far, far away from her mind.

"And that's what he always did, like sex. Sex made me forget everything," Farren admitted, after she told Mari the story.

"Girl, you got me crying," Mari wiped her face.

"You haven't cried as much as I have cried in the past few months, trust me," Farren told her the absolute truth.

"You have to move on. Don't stay if you're not happy," she encouraged.

Farren ignored her. "I really needed this, thank you so much," she told her for the millionth time.

"So what you going to do?" she asked.

"Pray and wait to hear from God," she said honestly.

"Well, I hear that, hallelujah! Now let's get me home," she joked but was dead serious at the same time.

After Farren dropped Mari off at home, she wasn't quite ready to rush home knowing her house was empty. Her sister-in-law had the children and she just didn't want be to home alone.

Farren drove through the city with everything on her mind. She knew she could do better. She believed that love still existed but who wanted to start over at damn near forty? Her phone rung and AGAIN it was Robin. "Girl, is that you turning on 44th Avenue?" she asked.

Farren locked her doors and looked around. "How and why do you know that?" she questioned. Robin was starting to creep her out.

"Just leaving my boo's house. What you doing out this late?"

"Dropping a friend off at home"

"Oh, so you had time to hang with your other friends, but not the one who saved your life?" Robin all of a sudden snapped.

"Whoa, whoa, whoa, you apparently had too much to drink. So let me let you clear your head. Enjoy your night," Farren told the deranged person on the other line and hung up. She then went to block her number. She was too grown to be arguing with another grown ass female. The only people she yelled at were her children and that was barely.

Farren found herself in front of her mother's neighborhood and she didn't know why. She hated her mother that much was true. But yet, tonight she felt like she had no one and all she needed was a hug from her mom. Farren felt her palms getting sweaty when she walked through The Courtyard. So many memories had been made there. She fought in The Courtyard, learned how to jump rope, and got her belly button pierced, all in The Courtyard. Farren missed her childhood just a little bit but her struggles, her setbacks, her fears and failures, even her flaws molded her into the amazing woman she is now. People shouted out from their balconies.

"Lil' Farren girl? Omg! Come here," one woman shouted.

"Marcy? Marcy is that you? Oh my lord!" Farren jogged to apartment D23. She hadn't seen Marcy in years.

It was damn near one in the morning and The Courtyard was just now coming alive.

"Girl, when did you get this ass and these hips?" Marcy asked.

"After three children and a fine husband," she laughed and slapped five with the other women siting on the balcony.

"Baby, we are all so proud of you. We saw you on the news with that there case. Now Farren you, be careful," one of the older ladies told her.

"Yes ma'am, I am. How y'all been doing?" she asked, taking a seat on one of the crates.

Farren hadn't chopped it up in so long. When she was little, her and Ashley used to sit out here for hours, literally all day and especially in the summer. They would get a bag of hot Cheetos and a pickle and just sit and watch the activity in The Courtyard.

"Good, just trying to make it out here. Hardy has changed since y'all were lil' girls," Marcy said. She still looked good after all these years.

"You know I ran back into Johan. We been kicking it, me and his wife," she told Marcy.

"Yeah, his brother just got out of jail not too long ago; threw a big ass barbecue out here," she said.

"Hmm, I didn't know that"

"Girl, your mama the one made all the sides," someone else spoke.

"Now if ma can't do nothing else, she can cook" she laughed. It's been so long since Farren had her mother's cooking. She needed to make her way over there, although her mom was probably just sitting on the couch with a colt 45.

"Y'all let me go holler at that crazy lady upstairs" Farren stood.

"You know she saw you when you walked through. Ms. Nakia know everything go on in this here Courtyard." Marcy was telling nothing but the truth.

When Farren was younger, all the major dope boys used to pay her mama to put their drugs and guns under our mattresses, as dangerous as it sounds. Farren used to think it was cool, til one day she was running her mouth and they got robbed. And the drug dealer, Big Rob, beat her mama down in the middle of The Courtyard, accused her of being a junkie and everything. She felt so bad, she really did. But not once did she tell her mother it was her fault. She was a lil' devil back then. Farren convinced herself to believe that was her whooping for beating her ass all the time for no reason.

"Marcy, walk me to my mama house?" Farren asked.

"Your mama mad at me girl, I'll walk you halfway," she said.

"Here," Farren handed her a stack of hundreds.

"Girl if you don't put that money up," she handed it back.

"No take it, seriously. You done saved my ass plenty of times and you and I both know it." Farren looked at her in her eyes. What her lips didn't move to say, Marcy already knew what she was talking about.

"I never expected nothing from you, I just wanted you to get out of Hardy and never look back, and you did. I'm so proud of you girl," she told her with tears in her eyes and a toothless smile. Years of doing drugs and drinking casually had caught up with old Marcy, but she still had that ass and that amazing personality.

"Thank you for everything." Farren hugged her tight, before taking the steps to her mother's apartment.

"Jesus be with me," she said aloud. Her mother opened the door with a scowl. "Ain't no Jesus in here, bring your ass in here," she said.

Farren shook her head; her mother had not changed at all. "Hello to you, too, mother dearest." She looked around and everything was still the same, minus the new television screen Farren bought her for Christmas. Her mother insisted on keeping the same tattered couch, claiming that after a long day at work she didn't want to come home to no stiff couch.

"What you doing down there talking to Marcy's drunk ass?" her mother asked.

"Leave Marcy alone ma, you know that lady love me," she told her mother.

"Mmm hmm, she need to pay her damn rent, always down there with all them niggas over there," her mother said, standing at the window looking over The Courtyard.

"Your sister told you I said your husband been over here? Them lil' niggas like to shot his ass dead," she said.

"I don't get into Christian's other business and you know that."

"I don't see why not. Your kids in that house with his crooked ass," Ms. Nakia fussed. She was as real as they came, Ms. Nakia knew all the original gangster's and in her eyes, Christian Knight was one of the fakest "connect's" she had ever seen in her years fifty-seven years of living.

"Ma, please do not call my husband crooked," Farren laughed. Her mama swore she was the realest woman living. Her mama was crazy as hell.

"What's up lil' girl, cus I got work in the morning." Her mother wasn't about to beat around the bush. Farren never stopped by so she was curious to know what she wanted.

"I think I'm about to divorce Chrissy." She laid her head back on the couch.

"Good," her mother said.

"What you mean good, ma? That's not good...I feel worse than I did when Dice died."

"Please don't compare my sweet Dice to that sorry ass husband of yours," she threw her hand up.

Farren's mom loved Dice. She didn't care for Christian because she felt like he encouraged her to not to talk to her family, instead of trying to fix the problem. His family came in and stole Farren from her. But in all actuality, Farren left her family on her own.

"Your sweet Dice?"

"If nothing would have happened to Dice, y'all would have still been together and you know it."

"Ma, not if he wasn't leaving his wife. Oh no ma'am, I would have moved on." That was one thing they never just really discussed. Her mother encouraged her relationship with Dice, because in her eyes, he did no wrong.

"Girl save that shit for them lil bourgeois friend of yours," she lit a cigarette.

"Let me head to my side of town. I had fun tonight in ole Hardy." Farren stood and stretched. Her mama really needed a new couch.

"You ain't cook?" she walked into the tiny kitchen.

"Girl, hell nah I ain't cook. get out my kitchen" she yelled.

"Let me get out of here, crazy lady. I left some money in your cookie jar. Don't spend it all in one place," she told her mom.

"It's too late for you to be carrying large amounts of cash"

"This my hood, I'm good." She patted herself down to signify she was the woman around Hardy.

"Thank you for stopping by. You getting fat, I ain't seen you," she teased.

"This what good eating do to you," she joked back.

"Farren, you be in that big ass house cooking?"

"Yes ma'am. Mama I be throwing down all the time, every night. I made greens, turkey necks and everything, and I got a garden," she bragged.

"A garden? You don't say. I always said when they tear down Hardy I'ma get me a house so I can plant me some cabbages and squash." She rubbed her knees as she sat down on the couch.

"Ma, you need to move from over here. It's getting worse and worse" she complained.

"Girl my mama lived in Hardy and I raised my kids in Hardy. You's a lawyer and your sister a nurse, about to be a doctor. I did damn good," she praised her own parenting skills. Farren didn't want to rain on her parade, so she said nothing.

"Let me go, it's late. I got work in the morning," she said once more.

"Bring my lil' snobby grandkids to see me one day. I ain't seen that lil' one yet."

"Noel, ma, she me all over again, honey. I will," Farren told her mom, and she meant it, honestly. Life is short and in the end, if she was to leave her husband or if her husband was to leave her, she really had nobody.

Farren walked to her truck, saying goodbye to everybody in The Courtyard.

"Twice in one day? This gotta be a sign," Jonte said. He was watching a dice game. "Why are you out so late? And shit, like this is dangerous," she pointed to the dice game.

"Bad habit," he told her.

"Mmm hmm, I bet," Farren told him. She switched her purse from one shoulder to the other.

"You still looking pretty."

"It's been a long day, I know I look crazy now," she told him.

"Nah you looking good. I like the lil' corporate look on you."

She smiled, "walk me to my car" she told him without asking.

"Yo spider, I'll be right back," he told his partner, she assumed.

"Why you out this late?" he asked her.

"I haven't seen my mama in about seven years. I just wanted to see her face," she told him.

"Seven? Damn Farren, that's not wasup."

"I know. I'm trying to fix it now, trust me." She felt so bad that she's been harboring grudges that long.

"Do that," he told her, opening her door, after she unarmed the vehicle.

"Get home safe. Let me get your number so I can text you and make sure you got home safe," he tried to slide in.

"Nah, I'm good. My husband at home waiting on me," she told him.

"You sure about that?" he asked, not in a sarcastic tone but in a "I don't think so" way.

"Why you say that?"

"I just left the strip club cus the bitches in there was whack and he and his peoples were in there," he told and didn't give a fuck. Jonte really wanted Farren.

"Oh okay, well let me get home before him then," she said, rolled her window up and pulled off, leaving Mr. Sexy standing alone.

Farren wasn't even mad at Christian. She was too sleepy to be angry. Tomorrow, she had another long day ahead of her. Being mad at a man who had no desire to change or no fight to save their marriage was pointless. If he didn't care, then damn, she didn't care either. Farren felt this way now, but she knew once she got home, she would be tossing and turning, missing her husband.

She called his phone and didn't receive an answer. Farren drove home in silence; her mind was completely filled with all kinds of thoughts.

Christian

"Y'all boys get home safe," Christian told his crew. They had been celebrating Ramone's death and flossing in the streets. Greg felt like the team needed to step out and show people that they still running shit.

However, for a man in Christian's position, his ass should have been home. It was unprofessional and dangerous for him to be out in public, with men who he didn't even know if he could trust or not. Christian should have transferred all his "mourning and celebrating" energy and placed it into locating the rat.

If he would have had really been on his P's and Q's, he would have known that there were a few things off about the strip club tonight. Christian never noticed the federal agents sitting at the bar. They didn't even attempt to conceal who they were. They wanted Christian to know that they were on his ass like white on rice.

Christian also should have picked up on the vibe in the club. For it to be an Amateur Night, the club wasn't really popping, and that was weird. He never noticed the few men eye balling him with black hoodies on. Christian was too busy smoking blunts back to back, and keeping his eye on Asia. He was losing his touch and that 'wisdom" that so many people wish they had, he didn't even apply it to real life situations.

Christian and Asia crossed the street to their car, and didn't even notice the young boy walking up behind Christian with the baseball bat in his hand.

"BOW!!" Christian went down in 2.5 seconds. Asia was so busy posting pictures on social networks, she wasn't aware of her surroundings. She looked up and screamed, dropping her cell phone on the cement.

Greg heard a scream and instantly thought of Christian. He took off running in the opposite direction with his gun in his hand.

"I'm okay," he mumbled, minutes later.

"Asia, you sure you didn't see nothing?" Greg asked her for the millionth time. This story just didn't add up to him.

"No I didn't, I was texting," she repeated. Christian sat at the bar of the club. They escorted him back in there to deal with his throbbing headache.

"Farren would have never been on her phone while y'all walked to the car, what the fuck!" he spat.

"Hey man, watch it" Christian warned.

"No, you need to tighten up, you slipping," Greg yelled.

"Respect," Christian said, which meant he was letting the conversation go. He didn't like arguing with his best friend.

"You good? I'ma drop you off at the house, you don't need to be driving" Greg asked Christian.

"I'ma stay at Asia's crib tonight, bro, I'm good." He tried to stand, but struggled.

"Huh? Are you sure?" Greg asked.

"You heard him" Asia spat. She wasn't a rat but Greg had been throwing shade for the longest, and she was fed up.

"Get home safe, keep your eyes and ears open," Greg told Christian, but looked dead at Asia as he spoke.

He didn't like that bitch at all.

When they left, Greg had one of the workers follow them home to make sure they made it safe.

"A bat though, my nigga? They didn't try and kill him that was just a warning," Jeremiah said.

"Exactly" Greg replied, but he was really deep in thought. This new bitch was going to be Christian's downfall and as close as they were, only God knows the dirt they had done together. He would never let anyone interfere with his money.

Greg was way more focused then Christian. He played many roles; the dealer, the supplier, the enforcer, the counselor, the lieutenant and the boss. Niggas that were in the street didn't even know who Christian was. Greg was the one that was really known as "THE CONNECT".

Asia asked Christian the next morning, "what's wrong with your friend? What did I do to him?"

"Greg? He's just protective of Farren, don't take it personal," he told her.

"How am I not to take it personal? What happens when we get together? Your family and friends have to accept me. I'm not Farren," she said.

"When we get together? Huh? What you talking about?" he asked. Asia was taking him too fast. His head was still spinning and she wanted to discuss their "relationship".

"Y'all are getting a divorce right?" she asked.

"Okay, time out, time out. At first you was happy with how things were, now all of a sudden it's when am I getting a divorce? I don't like pressure" he said, removing the covers off of him to go to the bathroom.

"You continue to contradict yourself. One day it's I can't wait to be with you, now today it's Asia shut the fuck up and don't ask me no questions," she yelled.

"Why are you yelling? We can have a civil conversation without yelling," he told her. Christian was a calm man, a very calm man and all that yelling and fussing isn't how he operated. If he wanted to be yelled at early in the morning, he would have gone home last night to nagging ass Farren. Asia said nothing, and for that he was grateful. Christian was so caught up in showering and getting dressed to begin his work day, he never noticed the sad face that Asia had.

"I'll holler at you later." He grabbed his car keys off of the dresser and left the apartment.

Asia wiped the tears from her face and told herself to not be dramatic and just stay in her place. She loved Christian and he adored her chilled manner and how laidback she was. Asia needed to stay that way before she lost her man.

Farren

Her love for her husband was not to be confused or twisted; she cried every night. Farren had begun to spend a lot of time with Mari and she deemed herself to be a very loyal friend. She encouraged her to do what was best for her and her children. Farren became an investigator at night. She would pull her pen and pad out, and have her calendar nearby. She went back to their bank statements, looking for hotel confirmations and rental cars. She had to get to the bottom of this mess. She attempted to see where the passion, love and lust went. Christian respected her, but he cheated, and Farren needed to understand why. It was the one question she desperately needed the answer to.

It was another late night and Farren couldn't sleep. After tossing and turning, she came to the realization that it was hard for her to sleep without Christian being in the bed with her. She crept to the movie theatre located in the basement of their home and watched their wedding for the millionth time. She fast forwarded up until they got to the part where it was time for her to enter the church.

Farren entered the church to Luther Vandross', "Here and Now". Her father escorted her down the aisle. Farren wore a custom-made dress. She barely ate this week to make sure she fit it in perfectly. Their wedding was planned a year prior to the date with Farren planning their wedding on her own. Christian told her she was stressing herself out and needed to hire a coordinator, but she believed no one could bring her vision for her dream wedding to life like she could. Millions of dollars had been spent on her fairytale, and her fiancé spared no expense. What Farren wanted, she got. His sisters warned that she was spending entirely too much money, even their engagement party was over the top. Her bridal shower was extravagant. Farren's dress was flown in from Paris; the flowers used in her wedding were all freshly picked the day before the wedding. The jewelry Farren wore was special designed for her wedding day. She had the best of the best photographers and videographers filming her big day. Farren wanted every facial expression to be captured from more than one angle. She carefully did her seating arrangements for her reception. Her wedding was about her and Christian's union; she wanted no mess or drama. For that very reason, she didn't have a bridal party. Her best friend served as her maid and matron of honor, and Greg served as Christian's best man. Christian had tears in his eyes and his best man Greg hugged his shoulders. Everyone gasped as Farren approached the altar. Christian beamed at her and mouthed 'you're beautiful' to her. She had been with this man for two years before their wedding date, and *they had one daughter together. But seeing him today, seconds before they confessed their love before family and friends was a moment she would never forget. He hugged and kissed her before the pastor could even speak. He held her head to his ear. "You are making me the luckiest man in the world right now," he whispered as tears formed in her eyes.*

The pastor asked who wanted to recite their vows, and Christian had beaten her to the punch. It was his idea to have handwritten vows. Farren didn't like talking in front of people, so hers wouldn't be long at all. She believed that their vows were sacred and could have done at home amongst the two of them. But Christian claimed he wanted the whole church to hold him accountable if he started messing up.

"Farren Knight, my wife, my best friend, the mother of my daughter, my business partner, my rib, my spine, my heartbeat, my energy….Farren, you are a blessing my life in ways that you will probably never know. Before meeting you, I had signed off on love, but you came and showed me what real love meant. This connection that we have is one that can never be broken. I promise to remain loyal and true to you always. Whatever I done before this please, don't charge it to my heart, because baby my heart only beats for you. You mean the world to me. There is nothing or anything that will ever cause me to stray from our love, our marriage or the family that we are building. You are my guardian angel and on this day before all these folks, I vow to make sure you have everything your heart desires. I promise to protect you from any hurt, harm or danger. Through sickness and health, for rich and poorer, baby I'm yours. Even when you get fat and your body covered in stretch marks, baby you gon' be my tiger. I love you wife," Christian spoke so openly and passionately about his love for his new bride.

Farren was speechless. She wiped the tears from his face and grabbed the microphone. "Christian is so over the top, how am I to compete with that! But, Christian I love you and for every single day that God gives us to spend together, I will honor and respect you. You are my King and you already know you are truly my everything. I thank God for you every single day. I would not be the woman I am today if it wasn't for you. I vow to love and cover you." Farren couldn't say any more; her throat was filled with tears and she was overwhelmed with emotion. She loved her husband so much.

That was the happiest day of her life; that was their best year together ever. They traveled all over the world and made a million memories.

Farren watched the video twice more before wiping the last of her tears and retreating to her bedroom. Even though tomorrow was Friday, she had a big court case in the a.m. and was praying for a successful close.

The next morning, Farren prayed before starting her day. She asked for peace, joy and happiness and also a fair and clean trial. She had been working tirelessly on this case and today the verdict would be read.

The judge was running late and so was her client. Farren had been calling his phone back to back since she woke up this morning and he didn't answer. She sat tapping her fingers on the wooden table, praying this man didn't do what she thinks he did. She had already gone through three coffees. Stressing at this point wasn't even a good enough word to describe how she was feeling. She sat at the table praying for both the judge and her client to show up. She was ready to get this case over with, win or lose. Farren smiled as she looked down at the silver and periwinkle Rolex she wore today. Her mind went back to when she received the watch as a gift from Christian. It was his "Happy 1st Case Day" gift. Farren will never forget how special he made her day.

"Baby, wake up!" Christian whispered into his wife's ear. It was seven in the morning, and in one hundred and eighty minutes, she would be representing her first case as Farren Knight, Attorney at Law.

"No, move man," she mushed him out of her way, after seconds of Christian attempting to wake her up.

"I made you my famous pancakes, baby, get up," he asked again. After Farren heard the word "pancake", she hopped out of bed. She loved her husband's pancakes; they were the bomb.com. Farren brushed her teeth and washed her face and met Christian in the kitchen.

"I knew that was gon get your ass up" he said laughing and placing a big stack of his infamous pancakes in front of her at their dining room table.

"Good morning to you too," she smiled.

"How are you feeling right now?" he asked.

"Christian, I'm nervous. You know I talk mad and I can't control my facial expressions when I'm irritated," she rambled. *Farren had been working so hard on this case she had no choice but to go in and beast.*

"You got this, boo. Come on and finish eating. I have a few more surprises for you," he said smiling. *It was the little things her husband did, which made her feel like the luckiest girl in the world.*

"Okay baby."

After they cleaned the kitchen together, he held her hand as they went back to their bedroom. Christian had Farren a brand new suit laid out on the bed.

"Oh my God, baby," she exclaimed. *The all-white suit designed by Prada and the cheetah pumps by Dolce, would have Farren looking like a billion bucks. Christian didn't just want her to feel like an attorney when she presented her opening argument, but he also wanted his wife to look the part as well.*

"And I got you this, too," he told her and handed her a small box with a yellow ribbon. *Farren ripped the ribbon away, and saw the iciest Rolex.*

"This is so playa," she told her husband. *He laughed at how hood Farren could be at times.*

"I'm glad you like it, anything for you my beautiful Queen," he kissed her lips.

"Damn, can I get some of this pussy before you go to court,"
he said, pulling her shorts down.

"Nooo daddy, I got you, I promise. When I get back we can
celebrate all night," she tongued her husband down.

"You promise?" he kissed her back.

"Yes baby." She smiled at him and secretly thanked God for
sending her such an amazing husband.

Hours later, the jury concluded and Farren marched out of
the courtroom in her grey pantsuit happy as hell, despite
the bullshit she endured at home. Her career was taking off
like never before; she was in the mood to celebrate.

Instantly, she was saddened. After doing interviews all
days, she realized she had no one to share her success
with. She called Mari. "How'd the case go? I been on pins
and needles since this morning when I talked to you," she
yelled into the phone.

"You must ain't been watching the news," Farren shook her
head.

"Hell no, girl, that shit depressing. So did you win?" she
asked.

"YES!" Tears of joy rolled down her face. Farren fought
tooth and nail in court, and it paid off.

"Bitch turn up, we going out tonight, it's on me! I need to
get out the damn house. I'm dropping these kids off as
soon as they get out of camp, so be ready at eight. I'll have
the car come get you," she said before ending the call.

She was happy that she had someone in the city to celebrate her accomplishments with her. She was always missing her best friend in Atlanta. She went home to nap before her night began. Farren was happy that the kids were on a retreat with Jack & Jill and wouldn't be back until next week. She didn't have to worry about finding a babysitter, or better yet asking her sorry ass husband. They were so happy to finally be out of school, but little did they know, mommy was putting all of them in math and science camp upon their arrival back home.

"I heard you won your case? Congrats are in order," was the text Farren woke up to and it was from a number she didn't know.

"Thank you. Who is this?" she replied before retreating to a bubble bath.

Farren enjoyed her bath with a glass of red wine and Jill Scott blasting through her speakers. She had a very long and emotional week. But with success on her side, she saw life in a new way and she was destined to place sadness and all that crying behind her. The front door closed and Farren heard someone jotting up the steps. She didn't fear anything while she was at home. The fact that they lived in a very secluded neighborhood kept her calm, and she knew it was none other than her estranged husband.

"Hello," he said when he entered their bathroom, pulling his tie from around his neck. Farren lunged deeper under the bubbles. "Hi," she managed to respond.

"Kids still not back?" he asked from his closet. She let the drain up on the tub.

"No," she told him, while wrapping a towel around her body. She checked her phone for missed calls and text.

Mari- I'm just now getting home from the hairdresser!

Farren- just got out the tub. I'm moving slow, take your time.

Mari- no dinner at 9. I'm rushing! See u soon.

The unknown number – Jonte

DON'T ANSWER- Mrs. Knight, your time is winding down. We just need one name. Please call us back.

Farren ignored Jonte's message. As long as she was married, she didn't feel comfortable entertaining another man. And those damn federal agents... today was her big day; she didn't even give their "warning" much thought. Christian told her he was handling it, so she left it in her husband's hands. She knew for sure that he wouldn't allow hurt, harm or danger to come to their family.

Farren exited her closet dressed for the gawds. Her hair was silk pressed with a middle part, she was dressed in a bebe black cross-out top and a red high waist skirt and black Celine pumps.

Farren stood in the foyer of their home, sipping wine and patiently waiting on the car that Mari sent for her for tonight's activities.

"You going out again?" Christian asked.

"Mmm hmm, yep I'm going out again," she told him, shaking her head. The nerve of this man.

"You got people coming to the house now? Farren you tripping," he continued to ask questions.

She looked at him. "It's a car service and I pay bills at this house just like you do," she told him before leaving their home.

"Whoa, whoa, whoa, when the ball drops that's when they realize...whoa, whoa, whoa," some rapper pumped the crowd up. Farren barely listened to the radio but she was turned up anyway. They club hopped all night, and her feet were now screaming to be rubbed, sucked and licked. It was 3:30 in the a.m. and she was ready to call it a night. Mari's drunken ass came staggering over with two shot glasses in her hand. "My friend won her case. This for you friend," she whined and kissed her cheek. Farren couldn't do anything but laugh.

She saw Jonte dapping a few people up. She watched him watch her all night. They both didn't speak, and she was confused as to why he sent bottles, food and roses over to their section but never approached. She told Mari's sister, Aaliyah, she was coming right back, and the bodyguard lifted the velvet rope and helped her down. "Whew," Farren exhaled. She had definitely reached her limit on drinks for the night.

She strutted to his section which was directly across from hers. "Why didn't you speak?" she whispered in his ear. He pointed to his ear to motion that it's too loud. Farren stood on her tippy toes and placed her mouth directly in his ear, and using her tongue and lips she asked again "why didn't you come speak to me?"

"You saw me just like I saw you, ma," he told her.

She nodded her head. "You right about that. Enjoy your night." She straightened her skirt as Jonte pulled her back into him. "Where you think you going?" She played his game. "I can't hear you," she mouthed back.

"Come here." He pulled her in front of him and fixed her another drink. One of Beyoncé's most popular hits came on and Farren instantly got in the groove. "This your jam, ma," he joked. She kept her eyes closed and sang with Yonce, "We be all nighttttt." She swayed her hips as he placed his hands around them and kissed her neck. She jumped back. "Chill," he told her. She made him spill a drink on his shirt.

She didn't apologize; she just went back to dancing. Another's man touch…another man's lips…how could she do that? How could she allow that to happen?

"We out", Johan told Jonte. "Let's go sis," Mari shouted and walked off.

"Come on boo, I got you." Jonte helped her down the steps and out the club. "Ride with me, I'll make sure you get home safe," Jonte told her.

"You know I'm married," Farren shook her head.

"What that gotta do with you spending a few hours with me? If you were my wife, you wouldn't even be in the club without me," he told her straight up.

"Maybe another time," she smiled, and flagged Mari down for a ride home.

"My brother gon take you down through there," Johan joked.

"And what is that supposed to mean?" she asked her childhood protector.

He shook his head. "You'll see soon enough. Stop playing with that man."

"I'm married." She held her hand up and flashed her ring.

"But not happily married, Farren. Just because you're married doesn't mean anything if you're not happy," Mari told her. She didn't know if she was just drunk or what. Farren didn't know how to react...to cuss her out or to hear her out. All she did was remain silent until they pulled up at her home.

"When we gon get to come chill out at this big motherfucka," Aaliyah, Mari's sister asked.

"Girl this empty ass house, whenever y'all want too." She said her goodbyes, pressed the access code and entered through the front door. Six bedrooms, three stories, movie theatre, finished basement, two master bedrooms, home office, complete library, kitchen equipped with everything you'll ever need in life and one unhappy wife. She trotted into her residence and noticed she was there alone. She called her friend Ashley and she didn't answer.

She even called her estranged sister and she didn't answer. Farren entered the kitchen and went through her briefcase looking to see if there was any work she could do, but there wasn't any. She was doomed and very bored.

So she decided to call Christian. After calling five times back to back, he picked up the phone, voice filled with sleep. "Are you okay? Is everything alright?" he asked, alerted and concerned.

"Yes, just couldn't sleep," Farren told Christian.

"How was your night?" he asked, yawning.

"I had fun. I'm drunk and bored, when are you coming home, Christian?" she asked firmly. For weeks she ignored him and allowed him to do as he pleased. She gave up on fighting him in a marriage he obviously gave up on.

"In the morning. Have breakfast ready," he instructed.

"No, I'll be dressed for breakfast at ten, and don't be late," she told him and disconnected the call.

Farren wrapped up on the couch in her favorite throw, erasing thoughts of missing her husband and his touch out of her mind as she slept.

The next morning, Asia saw that Christian was sort of rushing out of the condo. "I thought you didn't have anything to do today? You said we were staying in all weekend," she said, not nagging, just curious.

"I have to handle something," he told her.

"As in what?" she tossed the cover away from her naked body. Her skin was dark and chocolate but she was a sight for sore eyes. With no children, she had no stretch marks. Her teeth were straight and whitened, thanks to Christian. Asia was a certified dime piece. She stopped wearing long weave. After he told her he preferred a woman in the natural state, she donned a pixie cut.

"Breakfast with my wife," Christian told her. He scanned the suitcases that had begun piling up on the floor, for a clean t-shirt.

"Breakfast? As in a date?" she asked.

Christian exhaled. Finally satisfied that he had found a clean t-shirt, he tossed it on and went to brush his teeth. "Yeah, the kids are still gone on their trip, and she's bored," he said nonchalantly.

She cocked her head and bit her tongue, attempting to keep the peace. "Well y'all have fun," she said and exited the bathroom. Christian wasn't in the mood to argue. He promised Farren he would spend the day with her and until he made his mind about where he would spend the rest of his life, his wife came first and as always, what Farren wanted, Farren got. Not even Christian's new favorite downtime could change that.

"Are you going to bring up the divorce?" she asked.

He spun around. "What? If she brings it up yeah, but I'm not starting no shit with her," he told her.

"So wasup, y'all gon eat, shop, and you about to spend your money on her then fuck her and come to me tonight?" she asked.

He looked at her. "My wife is making more money than me right now, so knowing her controlling ass, everything will be on her today and I don't know what's happening today. I'll check on you later. Don't act brand new, you knew what it was from the beginning, baby," he kissed her forehead and left.

Christian was very careful to get in the right car this time. About an hour later, he pulled up to his home that the both of them purchased together, with clean money that they both worked very hard for. He texted Farren and told her he was outside. Minutes later, she was turning the alarm on and skipping a step two at a time. He caught himself admiring her, but she wouldn't see it through his dark lenses.

Farren's fragrance tickled his nose and he smiled when she got in the truck. "You look beautiful," he told her. She reached over and kissed his cheek. Together the couple headed to New York for the day. They always said once the kids got older that's where they were moving to. They owned a one bedroom condo that they often escaped to on the weekends when work was becoming too much of a hassle.

Farren talked more than Christian did, filling him on everything at work and the cases she was winning. He was in complete awe of his wife. "Whenever you wanna get your own firm, we can do it bae, just let me know" he told her. Farren worked hard and she deserved all of the blessings she was receiving.

"I've been thinking about it. We will talk about that later," she told him. Christian left the truck at the valet stand and entered Dantanna's for lunch.

Christian stepped aside and let Farren follow the waitress first. She wore a one shoulder emerald dress that hugged her curves and fit just right. Her gold Giuseppe sandals looked comfortable and she wore her hair in a bun with no makeup, just like her husband liked it.

"I need to get my ring cleaned," she whined as they shared appetizers.

"I'll take it next week, just leave it on the nightstand," he told her.

"So how is Asia?" Farren asked. Christian looked at her. "Eat your food"

"I'm just curious. Did she mind me having you for today?" Farren asked.

"I'm not about to disrespect you Farren, so what do you want to do after we leave here?" he asked in a very serious tone.

"Have sex," she said in the same serious tone.

He laughed. "You are something serious," he said, shaking his head.

The couple ate lunch rather fast since Farren was up front about what she wanted to do with her husband for the rest of the day.

Approximately one hour later, Christian's truck pulled up into the building where the condo they rarely visited was located.

Unbeknownst to the two, they were being watched.

Robin was crouched down in an unmarked car, trying to take as many pictures as she could, once they were out of her sight. She phoned her boss. "Agent Carter checking in; looks like the couple has reconciled."

The head agent on the case remained silent on the phone.

"Boss, what do you want me to do?" She was growing tired of following Farren every day. She prayed for the day this case came to an end.

"You can go for now. I will be in touch," the person said then the call disconnected. Robin, whose real name was Sondra, cranked her car up and pulled off. She was in desperate need of a drink.

"Yo, the agent just pulled off. That bitch gotta be a rookie. She is not discreet at all," an unknown voice said. He too, was watching Christian and Farren from afar.

Christian's biggest mistake was thinking he couldn't be touched. He went around the town never really observing his surroundings. He was unaware that in the streets, the grimy streets, being THE CONNECT meant nothing.

"Something doesn't feel right. I feel like we're being watched," Farren looked around.

"You're being paranoid, come on," he hushed her.

Farren followed him, but she looked over her shoulder one more time, and that eerie feeling didn't go away. She didn't know about Christian, but she had her gun in case something popped off.

The elevator brought them to the private entrance of their condo, and Farren wasted no time removing her dress to reveal the white half bra and see through crotch less panties she wore.

"Oh, you knew you was getting some today, huh? Is that why we spending today together, so we can fuck?" he asked.

"You used to spend every free moment you had with me and the kids, but you've been occupied." She toyed with her nipples and walked backwards to the room.

"We can fix that," he told her, undressing quickly.

"You love me?" She asked, laying down on the bed and spreading her legs, giving her husband front row seats to the best show ever. Christian licked his lips. "Yes baby, you know that," he told her.

She got up and finished undressing him. Christian was moving entirely too slow for her. She dropped to her knees licked his dick on one side. "Well tighten up and act like it," she bit down on his ball. He winced but quickly, her tongue made the pain disappear. Farren sucked, licked, choked, and pulled on his dick, causing Christian to nut twice in her mouth, and she hungrily swallowed every seed.

He lifted her off the floor and went to kiss her. "You kiss that bitch with these lips, don't kiss me," she cocked her head.

Christian was still trying to catch his breath from cumming; he was getting old.

"Shut up," he said before attacking her mouth. Farren moaned. Christian lifted her leg up as they stood and rubbed all over each other, while he finger fucked her pussy. Farren couldn't take the intense feeling he provided her. She panted and tried her hardest to escape his lethal attacks, but Christian wouldn't allow her to. He forced her to cum over and over again before even entering her. Farren was on the prowl for love as they fucked. She asked him questions throughout their lovemaking. Christian bit her tongue and neck every time she formed her lips to ask him another question. He tried his hardest to focused on the pussy. Christian fucked her something serious, as she begged for mercy on her pussy only to find out he didn't have any. Their sex was amazing as it always was. Many men waivered due to lack of sex and affection, but that wasn't their issue. Farren knew when to call, when to text, when to speak when to just let him be; she knew his on's and off's, his ups and downs. She never failed to please in the bedroom; she was a damn good woman in bed, but still something didn't click… it didn't connect. Christian was praying hard on his way to get Farren this morning that when he left Asia's home, today would be everything he needed, to remember why he married Farren. He needed a sign or a wonder, to remember why he chose Farren; why she got his last name and no one else did.

Christian thought he would have déjà vu, and get his shit together. As he stroked her, his mind went to Asia and how much it would hurt him if he discovered she was laid up with a nigga. He would hate it if she allowed someone else to pull her hair and arch her back. He would deteriorate slowly if he found out she had feelings for another man other than him. He refused to look down at Farren when he nutted, because his face wore the emotion of shame and guilt. He didn't want to be with Farren; in fact, he actually longed to be back in the arms of the girl who'd stolen his heart.

An hour or so later, they laid together sweaty, both caught up in their emotions. Christian trailed the sweat on her back and rubbed her gently. She twirled her wedding ring and he wanted to know how she was feeling. He loved his wife and never wanted to see her hurting, that was the God honest truth.

"You think you got something to prove to me?" Christian asked.

"Excuse me?" she said, never turning around from his back rub. It had been so long since Farren had one of his famous back rubs.

"It was so aggressive," he said, referring to the sex they just had an hour ago.

"Did you like it?" she asked.

"I always do, but you were aggressive and commanding," he admitted.

"You've been sleeping elsewhere, especially with the kids away all summer. It's gotten worse I'm in that big ass house all by myself," she told him.

"Farren, I don't know what I want right now but I do now that I don't want this."

Boobs hit him in the face. If the conversation wasn't so serious, he would have prepared her up for round two, but they needed to talk.

"What are you trying to say? Are you confused? A stripper, Chrissy? Really? All we have and all we have to look forward to. A fuckin stripper?" she yelled. She jumped out the bed and looked for her belongings.

"Come back and lay down, baby," he told her calmly.

"I don't know why I keep trying. It's obvious you don't love me anymore." She walked around naked, and stopped to look for something in her purse. He assumed it was candy.

"We have to have this talk. Why do you keep running from it?" he yelled.

"You don't to get hurt or embarrass me. Fifteen fuckin years of marriage, three kids and you gone leave me for a stripper?" she turned around and threw a vase in his direction.

Naked and all, her body trembled. She turned red. The bun that was perfected earlier was now a wild mess over her head. Her hands shook and tears fell. Christian barely missed the vase coming for his head. "All you care about is what everyone else is going to think. Fuck them," he told her.

"What is your family going to say? What about your kids? I thought you didn't believe in divorce, huh, motherfucker," she yelled, ripping pictures off the wall.

"You don't care now? Oh, cus you got a young bitch? What am I not doing right? I'm cooking every night, suckin' your dick every a.m., I pay bills, I attend every boring ass functions, I've raised your kids, and I sit with your mother when all y'all act too busy, but now you wanna divorce me?" She continued on her rampage, shouting from the top of her lungs.

They've had plenty of arguments in their time, but Farren was submissive, she curled under Christian. She never talked to him any kind of way and just about bit her tongue to keep peace. On this Saturday morning, she was one fed-up bitch.

"Farren, if you knock another thing over, it's gon be your ass," he threatened.

She pulled her gun out of her purse and said, "Try me." She placed it by her side.

Staring into his eyes she told him, "I'm ready for whatever. I can't hurt any more than I'm hurting right now." Tears filled her eyes.

Christian looked sad that she was sad, not sad because he was hurting too.

"I love you and I still love you, and I'll always love you, but when I'm home, I want to be somewhere else. I can't keep living like this," he admitted.

She laughed. "Let me tell you something motherfucker. You think I wanted Carren? Well I didn't. I cried when I first found out I was pregnant. I wanted to finish school first, but you promised me I would be good. You made me feel like everything would be okay. So you know what I did for you? I sucked it up and do I regret my daughter now? Hell no. She bought me real joy. But I sacrificed for YOU," she pointed the gun at him.

Christian didn't think for one second she was going to shoot. He didn't fear death. He knew she was angry, but he couldn't be in two places much longer.

"I can't compromise my happiness so you can be happy. Why are you making me do this?" He wanted, no, he needed Farren to understand exactly what he was saying and how he was feeling. He would never force her to stay with him, if she told him he no longer made her happy. Farren wasn't being fair at all.

She didn't say anything for a few seconds. Farren was defeated. She nodded her head and left the room. Christian heard her moving around, and figured she was getting dressed. He leaned his head back on the headboard; in this bed, plenty of memories were made. For years this condo was their duck off spot. They used to come here and escape from the reality of the cruel world they lived in. He closed his eyes thinking about the good times.

"POW!" the gun went off.

Please Leave A Review

Join Nako's Reading Group on Facebook

Twitter: nakoexpo

Instagram:nakoexpo

www.nakoexpo.com

The Connect's Wife III is now available on Amazon.

Made in the USA
Charleston, SC
09 December 2016